# Cosmic Dust

AND

## The Eternal Code

\* \* \*

UNRAVEL THE ETERNAL CODE AND WIN CASH PRIZE

Story Holds Clues

All contestants must be 18 years or older

See Website for details:
www.CosmicDustCode.com

\* \* \*

# Richard A. White

# Cosmic Dust

AND

## The Eternal Code

## Expanded Edition

Helm Publishing
Treasure Island, FL 33706

www.publishersdrive.com
ISBN 0-9778205-0-5
Printed in the United States of America

# Dedication

To HELM PUBLISHING, for making my publication experience so painless and rewarding

To MY SIBLINGS — GLORIA, BOB AND ROSEMARY — for your strength and encouragement

To MY MOTHER AND FATHER — Bill and Lucille — for your tolerance and always being there for me, and for providing all that is necessary to keep me from failing

To THOMAS, my late brother, my dearest friend, my partner in life, for your counsel and wisdom, your thoughtful comments and insight which made me reach the unreachable, making this a better book in the process — without you this ambition would have remained a feeble flicker in a frazzled eye

# Acknowledgements

For encouragement and avid support, the author wishes to acknowledge James Suchy, Bob Andrews, August Tsanakas; Lucy Tsanakas; William Tsanakas; Bernice Bruno; Johnny Bosco; Frank Fiore, world's greatest jazz pianist; Mercia Fiore, author and vocalist; Gigi, Michele and Debbie; Jack and Evelyn DeFiore (author); Jackie, Sandy and Johnny; Shirley White; Jimmy White Jr.; Sharon White; Joan Vincent, Randy Andreoni; Renee Mitchell; Leah Anderson; David Siegel; Stephen Burns; Dennis Graber; Anthony Gillies; Major Richard Fleet, retired; Roos; Owen Evans; Mark Milbourne; Joan Vincent; Patricia Persico; Ron Smolen and the RSO; Phillip Dukas; Joel Seidler, Chicago's drum king; Manny, my barber; and Whitney Phoenix, whose classical-jazz piano style rocks Bellagio of Las Vegas nightly

Plus, **BOOTS RANDOLPH** — the best saxophonist ever to live; his music will outlive us all

Also, the **USO**, and all US service men and women, for the autonomy of a nation is in direct proportion to its fighting abilities

In addition, **THE TEA PARTY MOVEMENT,** and everyone in support of constitutional government — Go Mitt Romney… Obama, just go!

Lastly, **MAO TSE TUNG, PROGRESSIVE EXTREMISTS, ADOLF HITLER, CRAZY LEFT RADICALS, FIDEL CASTRO, MODERATE REPUBLICANS, EBENEZER SCROOGE, JACK BENNY,** and all other stingy, selfish, and unsavory people of the world without whom **ROBERT JOSEPH SMITH** would not have had the inspiration to come to fruition

"*Gazing up at the sky we ponder, we sigh. A well-ordered whole, we marvel and fly. In outer space dust clouds embrace, so many stars, the human race.... Children trust, elders fuss; comets flounder asteroids bust. Life's not always fair and just, in the end we're cosmic dust.*
—R. A. White

The following fable is a tale of "ROBERT SMITH," a frugal moneygrubber who, in the mold of the legendary "JACK BENNY" — will follow you in a revolving door and come out ahead of you.... The story of a man who pinches a penny so tight both heads and tails come out on the same side of the coin. A self-centered miser who, upon discovering the secret of eternal life, will share with no one, committing "eternal life" to code!

Good luck breaking the code.

# TABLE OF CONTENTS

Prologue ........................................................................... i
Chapter 1    A Sticky Situation ......................................1
Chapter 2    Hide Your Money but Good .........................8
Chapter 3    $1 Billion, Tax Free ..................................12
Chapter 4    Men in White ............................................21
Chapter 5    Men in Glasses .........................................28
Chapter 6    The Whispering Shadow .............................36
Chapter 7    The Lonely Rich Widow .............................42
Chapter 8    Robert the Atheist ....................................50
Chapter 9    The Shadow Returns ..................................56
Chapter 10   Sparkle the Magnificent ............................62
Chapter 11   On the Hunt ..............................................69
Chapter 12   No Dogs Allowed .......................................77
Chapter 13   Cash Talks .................................................86
Chapter 14   Sparkle the Musician .................................94
Chapter 15   Dirty Bird Sparkle ....................................99
Chapter 16   The Casino Robbery ................................103
Chapter 17   Meet the Boys .........................................108
Chapter 18   Black the Crack .......................................115
Chapter 19   That's Him ...............................................122
Chapter 20   The Eternal Code .....................................127
Chapter 21   The Convention ........................................133
Chapter 22   A War of Words .......................................138
Chapter 23   Sticker Shock ..........................................145
Chapter 24   Caught In the Middle ...............................154
Chapter 25   The Great Escape .....................................160
Chapter 26   Epilogue ..................................................168

# WARNING, ALL LIBERALS:

Be on the lookout for success in America; it's beginning to rear its ugly head....

The first six pages are aimed at political satire, after which a transformation, a metamorphosis if you will, will rise up from icy waters and, without awakening Godzilla, mutate into sci / fi wit and humor and — while stimulating the specific brain mechanism responsible for sidesplitting laughter — clip, snip, and rip sides.

Be advised.

## PROLOGUE

**"B**ARACK HUSSEIN OBAMA...HMM, HMM...HMM...!"

**"'YES, WE CAN!'** LOSE OUR JOBS!"
**"'Yes, we can'** lose our homes!"
**"'Yes, we can'** hope for change." But let's get it *right* this time, huh? Not this phony bologna nonsense, this **"Hope and Change"** doo-doo.

It's all a joke, right?

Whatever happened to the real deal, **"Hope and Change"** *we can believe in?* Where did it all go? Instead we get more of the same — something branded, packaged, and sold. Instead we get **"Hope and Change"** as defined by *Willard's New World College Dictionary...*

## HOPE AND CHANGE:

BARACK OBAMA GAS; A VAPOR LNKED TO INCREASED RISK OF NOSEBLEEDS, DIARRHEA, FATIGUE, SHORTNESS OF BREATH, BRUISING, AND HAIR LOSS! SYNONYMOUS WITH *HOPE AND CHANGE* IS 'OBAMA FLATULENCE'; FUMES THAT WAFT THROUGH THE AIR LIKE WINGS ON TACOS AND REFRIED BEANS.

"PRESIDENT OBAMA, PRESIDENT OBAMA — WE HAVE A problem....!"

"What is it, Tim? What's the *problem*?"

"The problem O Special One, whose sweat is the nectar of the bee, is we're out of ink and China won't send any more ink until we pay down the debt...and we *can't* pay down the debt without ink! Oh, Exalted Ruler of the Free World, whose armpits are a spring day's delight, we don't *produce* 'currency ink' in this country. Not any more. The Bureau of Engraving and Printing is in peril. What are we to do, just WHAT ARE WE TO DO?"

"I, uh, world's greatest problem solver, will, like always, uh, find a way. Have trust, my little tiny Tim. Just remember, 'Yes, We Can,' 'Yes, We Can!'"

"'Yes, we can' O Anointed One, whose ear wax is the ointment of the gods.

The president drew air, his face contented. "I smell it! Smell it? Do you smell it, my lowly servant of the regime?"

"Smell it, O Great One, whose flatulence are the perfume of the White House?"

"Yes, smell it! Do you not smell it, my little boy Timmy? Nothing is more gratifying than the promising smells of 'hope and change.' Hope and change' is in the air!"

"That's 'hope and change,' O Majestic One, whose morning breath is the sweet petal of a rose?"

"Why, yes, my child Secretary of the Treasury. What did you think it was? 'Hope and change' is that which flows through the air, its aroma wafting like wings on a deep fried burrito.

"What's this?" said the president, his face alight with joy. "More 'hope and change'? Please, my little one. Don't move, don't flinch...don't even breathe. I have to concentrate. I must have *absolute* silence...

"Ooooh...ahhhhhhhhhh...!

"Best 'hope and change' *ever*....

"Problem solved!" my loyal little czar. "We need not fret over *ink* any further. Fate is on our side. Atmospheric conditions are such that 'hope and change' will soon get its tentacles round my brain, upon which wisdom will overflow and thus save us from calamity.... Here it is...I feel it! The answer of the ages! It is coming, it is coming — the smell of salvation is upon us. O' yes, what a rush:

"I, uh, world's greatest problem solver, will simply raise the debt-ceiling and, uh, place the burden on our sweet but most effectively brainwashed children, all of whom, uh, would lay down their lives for four more years of 'Yes, we can,' 'Yes, we can'...!"

"O Supreme One, whose Bodily Functions indeed function, I am beside myself, for this is *not* what I had envisioned!"

"Why, Timmy, my adorable little Timmy, you look depressed. What, not *enough* 'hope and change'? Affix *that* nose to my fanny, young man, and I'll give you 'hope and change' for a lifetime!"

"BARACK HUSSEIN OBAMA...Eww, Eww...EwwwWWW...!"

THE PRINTING PRESSSES WERE IN HYPERDRIVE...NOTHING TO show for it but debt, as President Obama needed enormous sums to fund his reelection efforts.

Too bad the money wasn't free. Each and every dime had to be paid back. Sure, might take ten thousand years, but — well — kids were resilient, and could handle anything...including the "Obama Debt."

A shame our kids had "no say" in the matter.

To be fair, not all was at the hand of President Obama as former President Bush too played a role, what with sub-prime loans and TARP and, least of all, Bush taking his eye off the economy and falling asleep at the switch. The only problem was that which followed: Barack Obama — an utterly gross incompetent. Stated differently — despite all our historic and formidable challenges, we now confront the defining moment of our core — Western civilization was in peril, and the survival of the free world lay squarely on the shoulders of "Dumb & Dumber":

Bush was dumb and Obama's dumber.

Still, things could be worse, as Obama could be a Communist Sympathizer. Indeed, President Obama was an avid supporter of the free-market system — a staunch, true-blue, down-the-line capitalist. As was Stalin! In fact, all communists were capitalists.

Just ask him.

Would he lie?

Compounding things were know-all politicians, some of whom were out to destroy Mother Liberty. As it so happened, America was systematically being transformed into the Former Soviet Union. The Russian people were ecstatic, applauding their socialist counterpart, their sentiments most clear, honoring President Obama on the Russian postage stamp.

Little consolation for our destruction!

No matter one's view, America was on a downward slide and the dollar was in trouble, collapsing like a bad draw to an inside straight. In fact, the end game was just that: to destroy the dollar and overthrow capitalism. All we had to do is spend, spend...spend.... If only our president would go back to the third grade. Even if money grew on trees, no third grader would allow such spending.

Nothing good came out of a federal credit downgrade. All it did was shrink the dollar, raise interest rates and cause inflation. Food, gas, air fare, collage tuition, and home loans were skyrocketing.... Why doesn't our president get it? Stimulus packages and bailouts DON'T WORK...! Case in point...all we got for it was a credit downgrade — for the first time ever, no less. Never in the history of our country has a president allowed a debt rating downgrade. That is to say, until now...until President Obama started running things. Any principled president of honor and virtue would be so humiliated, so mortified, so disgraced they, plus their entire regime would jump to their deaths.

*Last one to the bottom is the winner!*

With respect, Mister President, we're waiting.

Like the Monopoly Board Game, the playing card read: *Do not pass Go...do not collect $200....* In Obama's board game, the card reads: "*Do* pass socialism, go directly to communism. Do not collect $200."

**WE'RE BROKE!**

Incidentally, we're still waiting.

Apart from a credit downgrade, all we got for our money was another day older and deeper in debt. Still, you got to hand it him. He pulled it off. He really pulled it off (on purpose or by incompetence), destroying "capitalism" faster than the atomic bomb destroyed Hiroshima! In fact, $billions were wasted on commissions and committees alone. Here's a thought...let's take a page from the Book of Forest Gump: "Stupid is as stupid does," and have our president appoint just one more commission — an "Obama case study in 'stupid does.'"

Why, we'd save $trillions!

It wasn't long before heaven got into the act, dispatching a brief but profound message to our highly polished, highly artful, highly crass spend-our-kids-into-poverty Commander in Chief:

> "*LET HIS DAYS BE FEW; AND LET ANOTHER TAKE HIS OFFICE.*"

Psalm 109:8

Sill waiting!

HOW IS CUTTING BACK ON DRILLING GOING TO SOLVE OUR gas problem?

Any clear-thinking person knows Green Energy has consequences; namely, gas and electric. How could we continue like this, these exuberant rates? Between the EPA and countless regulations no one could afford hand-fans much less solar panels! Green Energy was a sham, all hype — "snake oil" people pushing a brain dead agenda. Meantime, everyone's going broke staying cool in the summer and warm in the winter. Soon we'll all be dead from the cold and heat and President Obama will have no one to sell "snake oil" to.

If we survive — if we should somehow survive — let's demonize the rich so they send all their money and best jobs overseas. Hey, why stop there? We'll decimate our living standards and income levels to the brink of homelessness.

If *we* don't, Obama will.

Shakespeare said it best: "A pox on both your houses!"

TWO OF FIVE U.S. PRESIDENTS UNDERWENT ECONOMIC challenges within the last thirty years: Ronald Reagan and Barack Obama.

While President Reagan came out smelling like a rose, President Obama simply came out smelling.

Really smelling, like "Hope and Change."

If it were just he, that's one thing. Problem is, when our president smelled we all smelled.

The contrast between them was stark, Reagan a staunch capitalist, Obama a staunch Who-Knows-What.

Be that as it may, Obama indeed inherited a weak economy. But so did Reagan. In fact, Reagan inherited more than he bargained for. Namely, "Boy Rags"!

President Reagan had Boy Rags to contend with — sole heir to the "Smith" fortune.

A dire circumstance!

If only things were normal; like the Reagan years, when "communists" were weeded out of government! Brighter times, happier times, when paid jobs were far and wide and fruits of labor shouldered the bills. Back when work was the rule and children the exception, Boy Rags an afterthought. When one Boy Rags knew his place and was neither *seen* nor heard. Thirty-years ago, when diplomatic haggling was the norm and Reagan was more despondent over Boy Rags than the U.S.S.R.

Thirty-years ago, when the *past* echoed the *future!*

A long time ago the economy roared and business soared, the tills overflowing. But good things never last, and soon sales took a dive. It happened suddenly, the moment some raggedy boy got into the picture, whereby appearing among the penniless. The penniless hardly noticed, assuming the lad was one of their own, blending right in. Everyone went about their lives begging and scrounging, when suddenly the parents pulled up in a big fancy car wearing big fancy clothes and laying out big fancy wads of cash. That was the moment — then, just at that moment — when everything blew up, the penniless fuming, the economy spitting and sputtering, businesses going bust. Soon Rockford was in turmoil, the penniless pouring into the streets; rocks crashed through windows, and hundreds of stores were looted. The systematic burnings of capitalist enterprises commenced and the city rapidly deteriorated into civil unrest. The boy didn't even know he was the culprit — the cause of it all. If only he had just stayed home. But he didn't stay home, his presence seen, scanned, scoped out, and enduring more sightings than *Elvis.*

The crux of it all was wealth, family wealth, Boy Rags soaked in cash. Essentially, the lad was pauper-gold — tramp-royalty — blending in with the impoverished, the impoverished gutted, trashed, and out the window. Failing to measure up, they, the down-and-out, left nothing to chance, taking frustrations out on anyone and everyone of money — a.k.a. *crème de la crème.* Once the smoke cleared, carnage was strewn everywhere, *la crème* checking into loony bins, their nails bare nubs, hair mere stubs — those sour-puss mugs.

Just how this could be…?

The Smith family, that's *how!* Last year, when the Smiths became members of Club Royalè! Who'd guess, a boy — a mere child — turning everything upside down.

What say we introduce him?

He's Robert Joseph Smith, a shaggy haired prodigy whose duds were at odds with family prominence.... Robert Joseph Smith — up on science and down on attire. A boy genius whose tattered jeans, baggy and faded T-shirts, and worn-torn trainers affected *tramp* status.

With that said, let us go now to Rockford, Illinois, and look in on this most unusual tyke....

Our story opens in August of 1988, when Reagan was president and the Minnesota Twins won the World Series — all seven games. When people had bright, smiling faces and saluted the flag...and had no problem with "God" in the Pledge. Nineteen-eighty-eight, when taxes were low and Government stayed out of our lives.... Back when any given experiment could come crashing down on any given visitor at any given moment....

# Chapter 1
## A STICKY SITUATION

TREES SWAYED IN A MUGGY ZEPHYR, THE DOG DAYS OF summer upon them.... Thomas drove the car sticky wet, the city plain as a glazed donut without the glaze. He had this dull and listless expression, like watching weeds grow. Alice sat opposite her husband, the day routine as routine could have it; her expression was a *testament* of dull and listless. Inspiration was dead, dripping with yawns. They'd been in Rockford since the dawn of time, and nothing has changed: wash pinned to the line, another store out of business, the typical town drunk — city sites one step higher than a wake. Actually, things really weren't all that drab. In fact, the city was rather charming and picturesque. It was the *same ol', same ol'* that did one in: *same ol'* neighborhoods, *same ol'* scenery...*same ol'* yawns. Hard to imagine Thomas and Alice having spent their entire lives there! Still, after seventy-plus years, how could it be anything but dull?

The day drifted into dusk. Orange painted the western

horizon, copper light stretching across city streets. They drove past a bowling alley on the left and storefronts on the right, and happened by Machesney Park on West Lane Road. The park was centered on a gazebo, currently hosting the U.S. Navy band, music spilling onto the street; flag-wavers took delight, their essence *esprit de corps*. Thomas paid little heed to the band, at odds over his coat and tie…his hot and stuffy suit…. If only he could stand up to his wife.

Thomas was drawn to a billboard: "JOE'S DINER" — STEAK AND EGGS, $6.95. He pondered breakfast, his dry toast and insufficient egg…and held out for dinner at the in-laws…. The car cut right on North 2$^{nd}$ Street, and Thomas, gazing out the window, squirmed in his seat, his suit itchy sticky: Trouble fell out of a clear blue sky the minute he got into it.

Thomas Smith was once the director of Jennings, which made various hammers and tools. His career spanned over thirty years. He'd learned a lot in thirty years, particularly about people and people problems and problem solving. Amazing how he and Alice still had problems. Who'd guess, after 42 years of marriage…? Apart from problem-solving, Thomas rather enjoyed the trite visits with son Bill and family.

*Same ol', same ol'*….

They sat at a red light, when Alice slid a look in Thomas's direction. "Aren't you glad I bought you that lovely suit?"

"Well…yes…I s'pose." *Act casual,* buzzed a voice in his head.

"You suppose? You don't seem all that pleased, Tom. What's the matter?"

"Nothing, really…" Thomas drew his shoulders up in a shrug, his pulse trotting just short of a gallop. "I'd just like to know why? I mean, why now? Couldn't you have waited until fall?"

"Why fall?"

The light changed, and Thomas turned onto Old Ralston Road. He really didn't care to get into it, for Alice almost always had the last word. He absently tapped his fingers on the steering wheel. "C'mon, Alice, my sweat is boiling…waves of white-hot heat are melting my brain!  It's a hundred degrees out there!"

"Oh, Tom, you're being silly.  It's ninety-two...and your suit is polyester."

For all practical purposes a goose nibbled at the back of Thomas's neck, his skin all prickly.  "Guess'll just have to acclimate."

"Now Tom, it's not going to hurt you to look good for once.  Besides, the coat makes you look younger — and smarter."

Thomas turned into the wide driveway.  He guided the car slowly up the drive, and rotated his gaze to Alice.  He winked at her.  "You don't look so bad yourself, for an old cookie."

The car taxied to a stop.  He keyed off the engine and Alice, studying her reflection in the mirror, said: "I must say...that salon does really great work.  Nicest perm yet...."  She patted her hair like a cherished poodle.

They climbed out of the car, and strolled up the walk to the manor.  Thomas swung his arms casually, his suit breaking smoothly, his silver hair glimmering beneath the dusky sky.  He inhaled mightily, exhaled slowly, his chest rising and falling evenly.  His joint-pain had all but vanished, the pep in his step short of miraculous.  He was magnanimous, a giant, his sixteen-foot-two-inch frame soaring — *he felt ten feet taller.*  Still, was 53 again, the suit making him 20 years younger.  Alice too was spry, for 71: her beautiful perm, her meticulously painted face, her in-vogue dress.  *Age,* she thought, *is just a number!*

They trekked through trimmed hedges along the thoroughfare, low grumbling traffic heard from the road beyond.  They ambled past the gardens, where warm grass filled the air and tree branches bent in the wind.  The sun had slanted sharply, the moon ascending through the horizon.  A stately house rose out of darkness, lights glinting in the downstairs windows.  Suddenly Thomas was drawn to third-floor window when — then, just afore the door — an enormous balloon burst squarely on his head.

*BAM!*

Thomas froze like granite, his youthfulness shattering, over-the-hill aches returning.  Something wet and sticky coated his face, plinking off the end of his nose like a faucet. Alice spotted the busted rubber pouch and flew over the rainbow, Thomas melting like the Witch of the West.

He tightened with anger. "Happy you bought me the suit? Why stop there? Buy ten more!"

Alice was too perplexed for words.

Thomas rubbed goo from his eyes, and had no idea what the goo was. He smelled it. It was odorless. He tasted it. Bathed in moonlight, he said: "Never heard of molasses balloons, have you? What, *water* isn't good enough?" He boldly looked up — *WHAM!* — right in the mug. The pouch shattered to bits, Thomas all covered in molasses, his bushy eyebrows flattened.

"What's going on here? Why is this happening?" demanded Thomas, his face red and swollen. He tightened with anger, his thoughts racing. He shook his fist at the sky. "Why me...?"

An extremely intense silence ensued, when a belly laugh grew in the pit of Alice's stomach; she nibbled the insides of her cheeks to keep from braying out. But couldn't refrain, losing it to a spate of guffaws.

Thomas shot a rather frightening look. "What's so funny?"

"I-I don't know, Tom; really I don't!"

"So you think it's funny?" said Thomas, shifting from foot to foot as if he had to go to the bathroom bad.

Suddenly a third balloon came howling down, bursting on the front stoop. Then a forth, hitting the pavement next to Alice, splattering to bits. Alice involuntarily pitched back when a fifth, a laser guided missile, struck her squarely on the noggin, silencing her laugh; goo clung to her face and floral-print dress, everything icky-sticky. She brushed away the broken pouch and the luscious perm that was, wasn't. She swiped at the molasses, curls clinging to her forehead in ringlets, the injustice so great she wanted to yell with fury.

Overhanging branches screened out the sky but not the wind, leaves scattering orderly about — strangely intelligent leaves, as if having gone to Harvard; leaves stuck to their persons like feathers to tar, and Alice, fit to be tied, threw off sparks from her eyes.

Tight in the throat, she couldn't find her voice. Thomas tried to suppress his rage, his face smoking. He folded his arms and absently tapped his foot, and snorted in disgust. Suddenly the foot tapping stopped when, like a rainbow after the storm, split a smile, those gray eyes gleaming for the first time that day.

Alice got all squinty-eyed. "So I see...my loss is your gain; is that it?"

"Sorry dear, I don't know *what* came over me; really I don't."

And with that, the couple braved the elements, lifting their heads to the third floor window when...

*Bonsai* below!

*Wham, bam!* — smack dab into both kissers.


THE BESPECTACLED LAD WAS UP TO HIS EARS IN RESEARCH, his problem twofold: ONE, uncovering the secrets of levitation, and TWO, energizing matter. At age seven, Robert Smith was a workhorse, his mind brilliant yet so far gone — one step from zero gravity and two steps beyond normal. People thought he was strange, teetering between the real and the imaginary...the natural and the wacko. In essence, the boy was cracked, his ambitions offbeat and off-the-wall!

Or so it seemed.

Doctors were taking bets, holding out odds the lad was precocious. From one physician to the next, when the results confirmed it — "precocity"! Robert had it bad, too — a condition in which the intellect matured beyond the actual age. Despite its "brainiac" advantage, precocity was abnormal, or atypical, hence making Robert abnormal, or atypical — a "typical" nutcase...! Still, wasn't discouraged, his IQ years ahead of peer group, his fascination one big *ooh* and *aah!* Small wonder he should battle the Unified Field Theory, fight out properties of magnetism, slap weightlessness silly. Dogged by work, Robert's eyes stung and itched with tiredness, his undertaking the "Ray" — integrating atomic mobilization into the "Ray"! To achieve his end, blackstrap molasses was indispensable...the very element that, just **moments ago,** fell down from the front stoop sky.

* * *

JUST AFTER THE AFOREMENTIONED INCIDENT, ROBERT turned to the last entry in his journal and recorded windage: 90° East; drift: 06.5 mph; temperature: +31.3 degrees C. He jotted down a few other things and, clipboard in tow, made for the window ledge. But when he got there his head went icy numb, for all his laid-out balloons were gone — vanished into thin air!

Robert gazed curiously at the ledge, when a nail biting noise prompted a nail biting flinch. He wheeled about, and the door immediately caught his eye — crashed open! He drew breath at his parents leading the charge, his grandparents bustling behind; Robert's knees knocked, his tattered clothes shimmying like a cell phone on vibrate. He cringed at Grandpa's night-demon expression, his burly frame cloaked in gummy old rags. The boy shifted his gaze to Grandma, her floral-print dress a wilted flower. He studied Grandma's dark and wildly explosive visage — like Madame Dracula having a really bad hair day....

Bill planted his hands firmly on his hips. "Robert, Robert... what on earth is going on here?"

Robert went pale white, his eyes swimming from behind the glasses. "It was a mistake, Dad, really it was.... Something went wrong, so terribly wrong."

"What went wrong? What exactly are you doing?"

"You see, Dad, before I can manipulate matter I must create a condition, a control group to calculate center mass...the effects of gravity on mass. I have to conduct a series of tests, and the balanced forces in blackstrap molasses is the perfect vehicle for establishing a standard of comparison. Any less and things could go bust."

They all stared wide-eyed, as if the boy had two heads. Thomas, on the other hand, was furious, fuming with anger. "'Bust,' huh? Like the balloons you *busted* on my head?" The vein in Thomas's temples pulsed angrily.

Bill wheeled into his father. "Please, Dad, I can handle it."

"Sorry Bill, I'm not through — out of the way!"

Thomas pushed forward, molasses squishing from his shoes. He took a deep breath and tried to relax his tension — the purple vein throbbing in his temples. Thomas struggled to bring the conversation on a plane he could understand. "Now Robert, all this may be clear to *you* but I'm on a merry-go-round. What, your 'control group' is to blame for all this? Is that it?"

"Not at all, Grandpa, not at all...! My experiment is premised on air to surface, not air to people — *particularly* the grandparent variety!"

Thomas narrowed his eyes, his lip snarling.

"It was an accident, really it was. It won't happen again!"

Thomas rubbed his chin thoughtfully. "Okay, fine...I believe you. Just tell me this...how *did* you get all that goop inside those balloons?"

"Simple, Grandpa...a solution dispenser.... It *really* does the job."

Thomas folded his arms, his face dubious. Robert looked up at Grandma, and saw a smile cross her face — like sunshine breaking through rain clouds. Her old self was back, and Robert felt relieved.

Lucille knelt beside her little boy, and gave him a peck on the cheek. "I want you to go outside, Robert, and pick up all those balloons. When you're through, hose everything down."

"Will do, Mom...will do."

# Chapter 2
## HIDE YOUR MONEY BUT GOOD

*R*OCKFORD *C*ITY *BIG AND TALL, COUNTRY LIVING GREAT BUT small!*

Rockford was founded in the 19<sup>th</sup> Century. It was dubbed Midway, for it fell *midway* between Galena and Chicago. By and by the city took its name from the Rock River, which ran clear through the town, dividing it in half.

During the Great Depression of 1929, Illinois fell on hard times. Thomas and Alice Smith survived the Depression, whereby Rockford *prospered.* Bill, their son, went into mortgage brokering, wheeling and dealing like playing the fiddle. Having attained great wealth, Bill purchased several acres of his own, thereby erecting the family home — a 7,000 square-foot mansion.... At its completion in 1981, Bill and wife Lucille pulled up stakes, bringing bouncing baby Robert into the world soon thereafter....

T<small>HOMAS AND</small> A<small>LICE</small> <small>SHOWERED OFF ALL THE MUCK AND</small> donned clean clothes, making their way into the dining room. Vinyl and laced cotton draped the table, embellished with white china and fine cutlery. All but boy Robert sat at the table, where sumptuous food was consumed and idle chitchat facilitated discussion…. Having completed the main dish, Thomas poured hot coffee into a cup, and waited for it to reach a drinkable temperature. He watched as Bill passed Dutch apple pie to Lucille and, though stuffed to the gill, held on for dessert. He leaned back in his chair and circled his belly with the flat of his hand, like rubbing a magic lamp. He cocked his head at Daughter-in-law. "Best ever, Lou. Those roasts of yours are getting juicier every time."

"Thanks, Dad…always a pleasure."

Thomas rotated his gaze to Bill. "So how's business these days?"

"Really great, Dad… Thanks to President Reagan, the economy is booming and sales are way up!"

"Sounds good Bill; keep it up."

"Intend to."

"Of course, now is the time to close everything out; all your stocks and bonds, your checking and savings — the whole kit and caboodle…! Take all that cash and —"

"Right, Dad," said Bill, dismissing Father in mid-sentence.

"Please pass the coffee, dear," said Alice, trying to change the subject.

Thomas handed Alice the coffeepot and pressed on. "Hide your money good, stuff your mattress with it…bury it if you have to. Listen to what I'm saying, Bill…if you don't, all that hard work is going right down the —"

"Thank you, *sweetums.*" She handed Thomas the coffeepot. Thomas snatched it out of her clutch and forged on, hardly skipping a beat.

"— down the tubes…! I'm only trying to help, Bill. Be smart and liquidate. Hide your money good…bury it deep —"

"Please pass the cream, hon…" Again Alice tried to change the subject.

"— bury it underground if you have to." He handed Alice the creamer and continued on. "You know, Bill, history has a way of repeating itself, and what happened to my dad could well happen

9

to —"

"Thank you dear; please put this back..." Alice gave back the creamer.

"— could well happen to you...and a whole lot of other people.... Don't be —"

"Excuse me Tom, be a dear and pass the sugar?"

"— foolish...!" Thomas whirled into Alice, his eyes burning red. "Now will you stop with the sugar, the coffee and cream? This is important!"

"Oh, Tom," said Alice, "isn't like the old days. Nowadays banks are insured!"

"Insured, yeah, right...! What about the thirties, Alice — the thirties? Forget the Depression? Listen Alice, banks aren't always going to be solvent."

"We heard it all before, Tom. You just don't know when to quit, do you? Bill's doing just fine without our help; now get off his case and pass the sugar."

Thomas's pulse raced off the chart, his complexion deep purple, like a sour plum. They dueled eye-to-eye, when Thomas grumbled a low, achy growl — "UGGHHHH!" He nevertheless past the sugar!

"Thank you, honey bun." Alice emptied a spoonful into her cup and stirred. She turned to Lucille. "That's quite a little boy you got there..."

"Yes Mom, we know. That's why we've decided to bring Robert up with a firm hand."

Alice was taken aback, her eyes expressing dismay. She recomposed herself. "A firm hand? What does that mean?"

"Means Robert will be taught a strict set of rules or all that talent will go to the wayside. Can't risk it, you understand. He might otherwise grow up a hooligan or something."

Alice struggled with feelings of disbelief, when Bill jumped in to save the day.

"Yes, well — *hem, hem!*" as he gave a throat-clearing cough. It's not like we *can't* afford to spoil the boy, just that too many youngsters are out of control and we can't allow that. Parents these days are too carefree with their kids."

"Is that a fact?" said Bill's mother, rubbing her chin.

"Yes Mom, very much a fact," said Lucille.

"Hear! Hear!" said Bill brightly, expressing agreement.

"Parents need to parent, not *kowtow* to whims," said Lucille, firm and direct.

"Alice, pass me the pie," said Thomas.

"What, strict about money?" asked Alice, ignoring her husband.

"We intend to provide Robert all his *needs*. Nothing more.... I mean sure, he'll get gifts for his birthday and Christmas, but other than that, no *wants or desires*...and no *money*."

"Alice, the pie...!" said Thomas, his voice cracking.

"That's all well and good, Lucille, but isn't that a bit much?" Alice again ignored her husband. "I mean, you might end up hurting the boy."

"How's that?" asked Lucille.

"Think about it...Robert could develop a phobia over money. He may well become a tightwad, a skinflint, some kind of miser."

"Now for the last time, Alice," demanded Thomas.

"A tightwad...?" Bill's expression was politely puzzled. "The main thing, Mom, is that Robert will be provided for. And should he choose science as an endeavor, better still, because I am prepared to invest in his schooling — thousands, *millions* if necessary. Spoiling him is out of the question."

That was the moment when Thomas shot in like five U.S. Marines all rolled into one. "You are absolutely, one-hundred percent right, Bill...stand your ground — don't give an inch!" Everyone gawked in Thomas's direction. Thomas whirled into his wife with temperatures back on the rise. "If I told you once I told you a thousand times — stop butting in! Bill and Lucille are doing just fine without our help! Now get off their case and pass the pie!"

## Chapter 3
### $1 BILLION, TAX FREE

T HE NEXT FOUR YEARS ROLLED GRACEFULY ALONG. IN
that time Robert never wavered, sticking to ambitions like words to
a page. Shackled by labors, the boy was drawn to the slave pits
night after night, his work ongoing, energy depleted. Fall of 1992
found Robert particularly exhausted, his body worn to a frazzle.

He'd been in the lab throughout most the night, his eyes
stinging and itching with tiredness. He drew his work to a close
and moseyed up the stairs, to his third-floor bedroom; he fell fast
asleep in his king bed. Snuggled under the covers, he slept through
the alarm. Suddenly his eyes shot open. He whirled into the clock,
gasped audibly, and leaped out of bed. He threw on his glasses
and, dashing into the bathroom, ignored the freshly laundered jeans
and T-shirt his mother had lain at the foot of the bed.

Meanwhile, Fred Howell, professor of English literature,
waited for Robert in the downstairs compartment, the compartment
sizeable, situated in the basement laundry room. Professor Fred
Howell leaned back in his chair, his feet up on the desk; he studied
his pupil's book report — a narrative on the Plays of Shakespeare
— when the door flew open and Robert dashed inside, his

briefcase in tow.   He moved briskly to the table opposite his tutor's desk and fell into a chair.  He folded his hands and rubbed thumbs together, and grappled with tardiness.   "Sorry I'm late...guess I over slept."

Mr. Howell removed his feet from the desk, and sat upright; he fixed his unblinking eyes on his student.  "We won't make a habit of this, now will we?"

Robert swallowed dryly.   "No sir...this will *not* become a habit."

"Good, glad we see eye to eye on this.  Well...can't sit around chatting all day, can we?"   The professor clapped his hands together.  "Today's exam will cover various passages, and all you have to do, Robert, is name the play and answer a few questions..." Howell rifled through his book, stopping on the Plays of Shakespeare.  He raised his gaze to his student, who was gathering confidence.  Howell scratched his cheek, cleared his throat, and began reading:   "*My horse!   My horse!   My kingdom for a horse...!*"

"*Richard the Third,*" said Robert. "Play Five of the Masters."

"That's right," said the professor, his expression rather pleased.  Howell gamely moved onto the next:   "O, pardon me thou bleeding piece of earth, that I am —"

"*Julius Caesar*...Play One of the Masters," said Robert respectfully.

"Right again, Robert.  And how did Caesar die?"

"He was stabbed to death by several assassins."

"Very good....  And *when* did Caesar die?"

"March...the Ides of March..."

"Excellent, Robert, excellent...."   Howell jotted something down on Robert's exam sheet, and again leafed through the book. He stopped on the sought after play.  "Incidentally," said Howell, "Mr. Cunningham tells me you learned geometry and differential calculus all on your own...  Is that so?"

"Why, yes.  But it was nothing, really.  Just a little something I dabbled with on the side."

"Oh, I see.  At any rate, *Julius Caesar* was a bit of a

throwaway. I expect they'll get harder."

"I'll give it my best shot," Robert had said modestly.

Howell read with feeling, like a 17<sup>th</sup> Century stage actor: "I have possess'd your grace of what I purpose; and by our holy Sabbath have I sworn to have the forfeit of my bond: If you deny it, let the danger light upon your charter and —"

*"The Merchant of Venice,"* beamed Robert. "Play Four of the Masters. Scene one, when Shylock warns Duke."

"That's right," said Howell. "And would you know the Act number...?"

Robert rubbed his chin, and pondered thoughtfully. "Act Three?"

"No" said Howell, shaking his head glumly. "You know this, Robert... Act —"

"— four! Act Four!" blurted Robert, just in the nick of time.

"Right...Act Four. And what did Antonio owe Shylock?"

"A pound of flesh!" said Robert, his confidence back on the mend.

"Yes, indeed." Howell added more comments to the sheet, and raised his gaze to his pupil. "You did well. No point in prolonging this. Read the chapter on Robert Greene — the complete works of Robert Greene. We'll discuss it first thing Monday morning."

"Yes, Mr. Howell." Robert slid out from the table and, picking up his briefcase, made for the door.

Before leaving, Howell piped up: "By the way..."

Robert stopped mid-stride, and turned about. "Yes, Mr. Howell?"

"According to Mr. Cunningham, your treatise on *Synchronized* whatever —"

*"Zero Arc Synchronized Poles...*a paper on linear propulsion."

"Right...! At any rate, you've been selected for MIT...starting this fall."

"Aw-right...!"

"Congratulations...you're the first *ever* to attend the Massachusetts Institute of Technology at the ripe ol' age of twelve."

Robert's face went bright, elation sweeping over him. He wheeled into the door and pushed through it, and headed into the laboratory.

ROBERT STOOD BESIDE THE CONCRETE SLAB, HIS JOURNAL clutched in his hand. He opened the log, and set it down on the weighty stone. He began to write:

> *Nonmagnetic materials can be levitated but only at the molecular level. Key to levitation is the solar chromosphere, which produces lift in a diverging field, stabilizing flow in balanced side-to-side projection. Only when the applied field affects orbital motion can external influences work to nullify weight against gravity.*

He read over his remarks, closed his journal and, tucking the book in the crook of his elbow, proceeded to the electromagnetic generator. He no more than set one foot in front of the other when his beat-up sneaker drove into the platform, the heavy stone unfazed! He let out a high-pitched yelp, muttered under his breath, and continued haltingly to the electromagnet. Once there, he set his journal down on the workbench, and turned to the generator, flicking a toggle. Low amperage resonated, and Robert gave pause to reflect on MIT. Until recently, he wondered if he'd ever make it as an inventor much less a scientist.

Not anymore...

Now that MIT was behind him, he was set free — vindicated. He could now search out the Patent forms submitted months earlier.

Robert mounted the hard wood box, and presided over his invention with stolidity, like a general poised for battle. He leaned into the workbench and took possession of the Ray — a handheld gizmo with a trigger and barrel-fixed-mount much like a hair dryer, except of solid steal. A thick cable connected the Ray's mount with the electromagnetic generator — a super-powered magnet, which transferred torque to wheels and rods without contact or friction of any kind.

Robert thumbed "ON" when the muzzle glowed orange, like electricity passing through a low-pressure tube. He set the Ray down and gauged the micrometer, low impedance emanating throughout. Suddenly the back door slammed, echoing inside the lab. A moment later Bill and Grandpa Thomas ambled into view, closing the laundry room door behind them. Thomas approached Robert with esteem. "That's quite an invention you got there."

"Thanks Grandpa. It's nothing, really."

Thomas turned to Bill. "What's holding up the patent?"

"Don't know, Dad. The forms went out eight months ago. Guess they're backed up."

Thomas rubbed his cheek, and chewed on Bill's words. "Yeah, well…maybe…."

The beeper resonated, when Robert pushed the OFF button and the Ray's glow dissipated. He disconnected the cable and stepped down from the box, shutting off the generator. Impedance faded, and suddenly the door at the head of the stairs clicked opened…. Lucille called down to the lab.

"Oh, Bill…you down there?"

"Yeah, Lou…what is it?"

"Got company…!"

"Who…?"

"Two gentlemen from Virginia…they wanna talk."

Bewilderment swept over him. He muttered under his breath: "Virginia…?" He threw his voice back up the stairs. "Okay Lou, send them down."

Two haughty-faced men in black entered the lab. They approached Bill with an air of confidence.

The head man seized the moment, also Bill's hand, and started pumping it firmly. "Hi...I'm Walter Lutz, Pentagon — Department of Defense." Walter split a twisted smile. He withdrew his hand and cocked his head at his partner. "Meet Glen Schaffer." Glen latched onto Bill's paw, and jerked it high and low like jacking up a car. "Science and Technology...!"

"Bill Smith."

Bill took back his hand and identification flashed before him. He gave their credentials a once over, and snarled his lip. "I see," said Bill, licking his chops like a wolf on a sheep farm. Walter and Glen felt something cold inside them. They wondered just who this guy was?

"So what brings you to *my* neck of the woods?" said Bill, his face foxy-clever."

"Just so you understand, Bill, we —" began Walter.

"'Mr. Smith,' if it's all the same to you." Bill set precedence for who was in charge.

"Right, Mr. Smith. At any rate, we didn't come all the way from Virginia to beat about the bush: If this Ray 'thing' does what it's cracked up to, my department is prepared to make you a generous offer."

"What, and keep it off the open market?" said Bill huffily.

"Certainly, by all means keep it off the market."

"Nothin' doing...! I am a U.S. citizen and I will *not* be intimidated by my government. Listen...go back to Washington or wherever and tell those people I'm not playing ball."

"But Mr. Smith, please...be reasonable!" Walter's voice oozed with earnest.

"I *am* being reasonable — more than reasonable."

"No, you're not. Really, you're not! Don't you see...in the wrong hands this contraption can pose a threat!"

"Contraption, huh...? I suppose you don't know a thing about it!"

"We don't know *anything* about it! At least I don't!" Walter turned to Glen. "Know anything about it?"

"Not a thing."

"Well then," said Bill, "A demonstration seems to be in order. If you gentlemen will follow me…" Bill turned, and made for the concrete slab, the agents close behind. Meantime, Robert donned a pair of protective goggles and took possession of the Ray.

Once at the slab, Bill looked Walter and Glen in the faces. "Feel free to examine the block. Go ahead, beat on it…" Their hands splayed all about it; they slapped it, pounded on it, kicked it… "No strings, no wires," said Bill. "No smoke or mirrors…six-thousand pounds of raw concrete."

Wearing shielded UV goggles, Robert punched the button when a low humming sound emerged from behind. The agents wheeled about, and gazed wide-eyed at the device. They shuddered to think of its implications. Just the thought of it sent terror leaping up their throats. For if it actually worked, the Pentagon would twinge in shock so deep and so blue, antifreeze would turn to ice!

Thomas handed Walter and Glen special lens goggles. "You'll need these." The agents put on the goggles. Bill said: "Please gentlemen, stand aside, for you are about to witness the most stunning breakthrough in gravity since helium."

Bill waved his hand at Robert. "I give you, 'The Ray'!"

Robert took aim and slowly eased back the trigger. A surge of electron beams jetted out of the muzzle, and wrapped around the stone. Seconds later a corona discharge sprouted forth, the stone rising slowly up and off the wooden platform, slats crackling. Three solid tons lifted up and away, *figuratively* falling onto the agents' shoulders, bones creaking in lieu of all that weight! Just then Walter and Glen offered a demonstration all their own, their lower jaws hovering just above kneecaps. They stood bug-eyed and open-mouthed, the concrete slab revolving over and all around the platform, demonstrating ability to differentiate evenly from side to side and top to bottom, like a hot-air balloon demonstrating a perfect balance of forces.

Although the demonstration lasted a few brief moments to Walter and Glen it was an eternity.

Robert lowered the Ray's muzzle, easing the slab back down

to the platform, settling back into position. He eased off on the trigger and, thumbing the OFF button, put an end to the demonstration.

A great terror seized the agents' throats, sweat standing thick on their faces.

Bill confronted Walter and Glen head-on, barely affording them time enough to remove goggles. "Now...regarding that generous offer...I too won't beat about the bush. I want one billion dollars."

Bill's words were sobering, curing the men of any and all shock. They whirled into each other and began a frenzied protest. "That's outrageous!" said Glen to his partner. "Nonsense, utter lunacy!" intoned Walter. Glen came back with "Blackmail! Extortion is what it is!"

"Tax free," said Bill from behind, *raising* the ante — and blood pressure.

Walter turned to Bill. "I wonder if I read you right."

"Tax free...! One billion dollars, exempt of all taxes."

Walter and Glen turned rigid, like mannequins, their faces flushed with stupefaction. Small wonder they didn't pass out.

"Come, come, gentlemen...we're talking pennies here. How can we bicker over pennies when National Security is at stake?"

"B-but Mr. Smith," said Glen pleadingly, "one million dollars?"

"That's one million with a 'B'.... Looks like it's time for a *powwow*." Bill turned to his father. "Dad, you and Robert wait here. Won't take but a sec! If you gentlemen will follow me..." Bill set off for the laundry room, Walter and Glen slogging behind, murmuring all the way.

Just as the door closed shut behind them, Robert meekly raised his gaze to his grandfather. "They don't seem all that pleased, do they Grandpa?"

"Never mind them. We need to talk!"

"Yes, Grandpa...?"

"Some day you're going to be a rich man — a *very* rich man. Now hear me good: never but *never* keep money in the bank."

"The bank?" said Robert, his eyes puzzled. "But why Grandpa...?"

"Banks can't be trusted, that's why! Completely unreliable! Let me tell you a story. Your great-grandfather trusted banks. That is, until the Union Bank robbery of nineteen-o-eight, when every dime was *swept* right out from under him. It happened suddenly, one unsuspecting Fourth of July day when guns ablaze were mistaken for fireworks, and Dad's money went riding off into the sunset. Trust me on this. Hide your money. Hide it good! Bury it if you have to. Just *not* in the bank...!"

"I see what you mean, Grandpa... I'll think about it."

"Don't just think about it — do it! I'm telling you for your own good, Robert — don't trust banks!"

"'Don't trust banks,'" said Robert, repeating his grandfather's warning. "Got it...!"

## Chapter 4
## MEN IN WHITE

"ON JULY SIXTH, NINETEEN-SIXTY-ONE, NASA SELECTED White Sands as a test facility….!" The tour guide addressed the young students before him, their faces captivated, hanging onto every word…. Jason Snipe, tour guide, was a black Southern gentleman with wire-rim glasses and blue NASA flight suit. He stood behind a concrete bunker, the air stiff but exhilarating, the class well attentive; Jason Snipe spoke with calm diction, like the retired colonel he was.

Kathy Hollinger took written notes, her pen speeding across the writing pad. The little girl was on a field trip from Bell Elementary — a public school 30 miles southwest of Johnson Space Center. The class teacher stood on the sideline with Master Sergeant Beasley, Project Coordinator. A sign read, "AEROSPACE TEST FACILITY" — BUNKER THREE. Kathy Hollinger inscribed information when Robert Smith — Nobel laureate — graced her thoughts. The sixth grade student reflected on *Futuristic Science,* the October 2011 issue, the write-up delving into the achievements of Robert Smith. While the article covered much ground, it made no mention of the Ray, as the Ray was strictly off-the-record. Since Ray negotiations, twenty years had passed in a twinkling of an eye...like an illusion at a magic show.... February the sixth, 2012, found Robert Smith no longer a boy of eleven; rather, a grown man of thirty-one.

"More than three-hundred and ninety rocket engines have been tested since nineteen sixty-four," said the retired colonel. "In that time, more than two-point three million firings have occurred. Just recently tested was Project Mach-up, a program aimed at the Ion Booster. To the success of the program, the Booster tested favorably, resulting in — well — in terms of 'supersize,' let's just say the booster has been supersized.... Now, are there any questions?"

Kathy raised her hand. "I have a question..."

"And what *is* your question?"

"Who designed it; you know, the booster, the 'super-sized' booster? Was it Robert Smith?"

"Why, yes!"

"What exactly did he do?"

"Smith retooled the Hall thruster...the entire propulsion process." The tour guide spoke rather slowly, affording time enough to write. "You see, unlike the power generator of yesteryear, we can now retrieve power from a beam of electromagnetic radiation...such as the sun, via laser. We can now travel continually through space on an endless power supply...." He turned to the young girl. "Does that answer your question?"

Kathy's pen stopped mid-stroke. "Yes, it does. Thanks."

"Well now," said retired Colonel Snipe, rubbing his hands together, "if there are no further questions, we will board the bus and head on over to the tram, which will take us to Mission Control Center. Once there, you may even get to meet Robert Smith. We'll then shoot down to Hanger X and the Space Vehicle Mach-up Facility; then it's off to the Shuttle Mission Simulators."

\* \* \*

THE HALLS OF NASA WERE BUSTLING, SIGHTSEERS everywhere — from White Sands to Mission Control Center.... A young woman from Arizona bumped into two gentlemen, one of whom was tattered and ragged, the other smartly dressed. She raised her gaze to the man smartly dressed. "Please, Mr. Smith, may I have your autograph? The spiffy-looking man twisted his eyes, and the other piped up: "You may, young lady, you certainly may." She handed the bum next to "spiffy" a pen and pad and tried to make sense of it, Smith's hair all-over-the-place, his blazer patched and four-sizes too big; his shoes were rough, scuffed, and needing a buff; pants worn, torn, and deeply in mourn.

CONFERENCE ROOM NUMBER ONE WAS REPLETE WITH spacecraft models and photos of planetary systems and galaxies. Sitting center room was a long and polished table, where table-cards denoted three **RESERVED** chairs.

Victor T. Map sat at the head of the table. In his late fifties and immaculately dressed, Victor Map — executive director — involuntarily shifted his gaze to the vacant chairs, longing for the Men in Glasses (MIG). The Executive Director drew a sigh, for the MIG would offer support — something Victor could use right about now; i.e., in lieu of things heating up between him and his flight director, Major General Paul Nicholson, USAF. General Nicholson sat all squinty-eyed, looking Victor in the face; Victor took a long breath and glared back. The general tightened his eyes, and clenched his hand into a fist. He thought, *Just who does this guy think I am, some ordinary civilian?*

Victor turned to the council in earnest. "I tell you men the design is ingenious, every detail flawless."

Nicholson jumped in with both feet on the ground. "C'mon Vic, you know more than anyone Smith's gotta loose screw. We can't chance it!"

"Lest we forget, gentlemen, Robert Smith is the *most* brilliant physicist in the history of NASA. As for his mental state — well — his mind was clear and sharp at the time of the project. Sure, *now* he's a little unhinged but, c'mon, we all go a little mad every now and again."

Eyes shifted to the general, expecting Nicholson to shoot back...but all he did was snort in disgust. An awkward silence ensued, the both of them dueling eye to eye, sizing each other up. Nicholson sat imperiously in his chair, like the King of Siam, and Victor tried to keep his eyelid from flickering.

The general finally said: "But we don't know that, *when* Smith became 'loony tunes,' that is. For all we know he was crazy when he laid down his plans — probably crazier then than now!"

The room began a steady stream of murmuring, and Victor told himself to calm down. Relax. After all, for all the anger he felt toward the general — whenever Victor had to choose between anger and the vision of his people — his people won out, hands down....

"Look," Victor had said candidly, "Robert didn't wig out until after the accident. Not before, but 'after.' He was fine during *PROJECT EARTH-TO-STARS....*" Victor spoke with conviction, his heart pumping. "I tell you men we're dealing with sound science!"

Carl Banks pounded his fist into an open palm; heads swerved into the man from Groom Lake. Carl Banks was head of Science and Technology, and he too yearned for the Men in Glasses. But yearn no more, as it was time for the wiry but distinguished Banks to make his pitch. "I can vouch to that — every word of it. In light of doubts, let me set the record straight: Each and every layout, all the design plans, every photographic print dissected...thoroughly analyzed by the greatest minds of Area 51. The results were staggering, utterly astounding. The laws of physics here is fact, and it'll work."

"Just *how* does it work?" asked Justin D. Meeks, administrator.

Banks rubbed his gangly cheeks, gathering thoughts. The distinguished body was the best of the best, as near to the halls of technology a council can be, and Banks had to make his case: "In short, gentlemen, electromagnetic propulsion that slows down time. A thrust system that warps time, bends light, and reduces space via regional fields of gravity. A pyramidal method that strengthens one system while all other systems strengthen each other! Processes working in concert to generate a black hole...."

They all stared blankly.

Banks sighed, and continued on: "Okay, a bit much, I know, but — well — think of it like this: an unbroken sequence, a reciprocal cause and effect. As time decelerates, gravity waves bend and oscillate, reducing space while accelerating at phenomenal speeds. A vicious circle if you will. An anti-gravity drive that warps both time and light, overwhelming mass and speed in the process...."

"I tell you men we're sitting on our ticket into deep space, and we *must* act fast!" said Victor Map, his passion flowing.

People surreptitiously glanced and shrugged at each other, and General Nicholson had seemingly softened his position. He said to Victor: "Pretty slick...the way you spun Smith's Nobel citation, that is. That bunk about the Ion Booster...really clever stuff."

"Wasn't bunk," said Victor. "Robert indeed made strides in Booster Technology. But hey, was all I could do. My hands were tied. I mean, nobody deserved the Nobel more than he, and since the world must never know what he discovered — what he really, *truly* discovered — I just see it as a trade-off, a wash: the booster for the *real McCoy.*"

The chief of operations, Clifford Campbell, tried to angle the meeting into a more jocular direction. "Anyone catch Robert at the news dispenser this morning?"

"Saw the whole thing," said administrator Justin Meeks. He glumly added, "Sad what's become of him. Isn't it, though?"

"What happened? What'd he do this time?" asked the general.

"There he is on bended knee," said Justin, "reading the Morning Journal through the window of the dispenser. People are trying to feed money into the slot but Smith's in everybody's way, and won't budge. Finally I tap him on the shoulder, when he stands up and glares at me with those eyes, those geeky glasses of his. I say to him, 'Just buy the paper, why don't you? It's only a buck!' Suddenly he turns all cold and dark, eyes tight and squinty. Says 'A dollar saved is a dollar earned...'"

The general turned to Justin, his head shaking. "Really sad... Guy's worth a billion dollars, too."

"Over...well over a billion!" said Victor.

"All that money and can't wear anything decent," said Nicholson. "Those waist high-pants and baggy blazer of his...went out with the miniskirt back in the Dark Ages."

"Don't knock it," said Justin, "miniskirts are making a comeback...the zoot suit might do likewise."

*"Comeback*, yeah, right!" said Nicholson.

"In any event," said Victor, "apart from one's frailties..." He turned to Banks and asked, "What are we sitting on in terms of speed?"

Banks looked at Victor for a mere instant when the door suddenly flew open, admitting three black Men in White (MIW): three orderlies from the Department of Psychology. The orderlies sauntered along the polished floor, their faces bright and cheerful, as if life was good. They marched up to Victor, when the head orderly handed the Executive Director a manila folder. "Pardon the interruption, sir...Dr. Moorland said you needed this right away." A wide smile split the orderly's face, as the MIW made it a practice to look happy no matter the anguish, no matter the pain. Any less could result in dismissal. Worse, shock therapy!

"If it's what I think it is, indeed I do." Victor removed an official letter, and read it quietly to himself.

The MIW waited for comment, some kind of reaction. They stood in good cheer, their eyes sweeping the tough, poker-faced men before them — men not afraid of hard work, not scared of anything. Despite the gloom, the Men in White smiled broadly, the council a dried up prune.

Victor raised his gaze with a stunned look about him, as if he'd been hit in the face with a two-by-four. A lingering still hung in the room. "It's official; we *gotta* let Smith go." His voice was quite, but it resonated through the silence. "It says here, 'Comprehensive exam shows patient suffers from delirium brought on by post-traumatic stress disorder. While patient's cerebral spinal pressure indicates normal, blood chemistry shows iron-deficiency anemia. A thalamic examination showed marked abnormality. Electro-encephalogram: atypical...'" He lifted his eyes to the council: "In other words, 'unhinged'!" He scratched his cheek, and continued reading: "'Undo stress will trigger unintelligible ramblings brought on by latent delusional tendencies. Diagnosis: type-one schizophrenia coupled with manic-depressive illness.'" Victor turned to Justin Meeks. "Mind telling him?"

"No, I don't mind. I'll tell him."

"Great...I'll keep legal abreast."

"Hope you know what you're doing, Vic," said the general. "...Appropriations isn't going to like funding some project cooked up by some whacko!"

"Don't worry; I *know* what I'm doing..." Victor turned to the MIW. "You're free to leave."

The happy three wheeled, and bopped casually away.

## Chapter 5
### MEN IN GLASSES

*T*HEY TOOK TO THE EXIT IN JOYOUS GLEE, SPIRITS HIGH *and worry-free.*

Suddenly the door shot open, when three Men in Glasses (MIG) entered in step and in tandem…gaits steady, postures erect. In contrast to the MIW, the MIG had long and gloomy frowns.

Life *hadn't* been good.

They all wore dark sunglasses, suits black and spiffy; they marched one behind the other, right past the MIW.

*Alpha Z, Beta Y,* and *Gamma X* settled into chairs next to Carl Banks. Justin Meeks eyeballed the MIG with an air of suspicion. "What's up with the glasses?"

Agent *Alpha Z* swerved into Justin. "For peace of mind, don't ask!" His words came out flat and listless, like a black and white rainbow.

"I don't like the tone of —" started Justin.

Victor gave a throat clearing cough — *hem, hem!* "Yes, well…" He turned to Carl Banks. "I believe the question is 'speed.' Just *how fast* is this system supposed to travel?"

*Alpha Z* whirled into Banks, seated beside him. "Don't answer that!" The distinguished council gawked awkwardly, and *Alpha Z* clarified his position: "Least not yet…"

Clifford Campbell narrowed his eyes. "Just who are you men?"

"Seated before you is *Beta Y* and *Gamma X,*" said Head Agent Z. The council gave them a once over. "I am *Alpha Z,* a.k.a. The Plumber…Groom Lake, Area 51…. We represent the New World Order, Majestic 12, and it's time we get something straight… What's said in this room stays in this room. Got it? 'Cause if you haven't got it you *will* get it…you will *really* get it! Top Security Clearance or no, I stop leaks. I, The Plumber, will 'plug' the leak!"

The distinguished body sat glassy-eyed, their heads swimming.

A humming sound suddenly emerged, when three horseflies entered the picture; the flies buzzed in and around the MIG, swooping down on pale flesh. The MIG seemed unperturbed, as if to have an affinity for insects.

Clifford jerked his head in *Z's* direction. "We're a professional organization, and I assure you men that *nothing* will leak —" He cleared his throat: "*Ughmmm…!* That is to say, leave this room. We don't discuss anything outside these parameters. Particularly black projects! But hey, things happen. I mean suppose, just suppose something gets out. What then?"

"Yeah, what're you gonna do, strong-arm us?" asked Justin, his voice dripping with sarcasm.

The MIG stared grimly, when chuckles broke out all around. Beneath the low humming and the buzzing, the horseflies too chuckled.

"What, you'll kill us?" asked the general, braying giggles.

The room exploded into full blown laughter, and the Men in Glasses just sat cold and lifeless, like three dead batteries. Through it all the MIG showed no emotion, no sign of hostility; no sign of anything, for that matter. The hilarity didn't let up, the council letting it all gush.

They hooted and howled with teary-eyed laughter, and suddenly three iron fists came thundering down, fracturing the table like balsa wood. The bang was deafening, everyone pitching back, the room dead silent.

Three fists remained cemented to the tabletop, and Victor grimaced at the hairline break in the wood.

*Alpha Z* broke the silence. "We will do what it takes!"

In unison, the MIG lifted their fists up and off the fractured table; they twisted their wrists, allowing mouth-access to fly guts. A brief pause ensued when, all at once, black and inordinately long tongues drove onto the meat, basking in the moment. The MIG slurped audibly, faces withering in disgust.

"Enough already!" said Victor, his voice snapping back in control. "We get the point!"

The MIG savored the moment, smacking their lips.

Victor Map brushed off the incident. "Now, where were we?"

"Speed..." said Clifford.

"Right, speed...!" Victor turned to Banks. "What exactly are we looking at here?"

"We're looking at accelerations to that of light speed —"

"The speed of light?" said the general, wide-eyed and awestruck. Intense mutterings erupted, and Victor tried to squelch the grumblings. "Settle down men, settle down."

The mutterings ended and Banks forged on. "The speed of light *squared!*"

The council turned to stone, their faces flushed with utter and complete astonishment.

Open-mouthed silence hung in the air, allowing Banks to press ahead: "An anti-gravity drive that will defeat mass, allowing speeds 'up to' three-point-four thousand, five-hundred and ninety-six to the $10^{th}$ power. In other words, gentlemen, 34 billion, 596 million miles *per second...!*

The silence was deafening.

"And now that Robert is essentially put out to pasture," Victor interjected, "our top scientists will pickup where he left off on inertia and force fields, and negative G protection.

HAVING JUST LEFT THE CAFETERIA, ROBERT AND MARY lingered in the hallway, trying to stay clear of the afternoon rush.... Suddenly a throng filed into the cafeteria, nudging them alongside the wall. Robert looked his usual worst, and Mary, who'd gotten used to it, hadn't noticed. She turned to him. "The food here's pretty good, wouldn't you say?"

Robert frowned, his face all bummed out. "Should've gotten the chili...!"

"Really...?"

"The soup was salty and the chicken's overpriced." He put his hands in his deep pockets and jingled change. Suddenly a man in a tan sport coat stopped before him. "Gee pal, whatever happened to you?" The man stood in gaping silence, his eyes glued to Robert's disheveled hair, his ripped and stained blazer...his baggy and patched trousers. The man patted Robert painfully on the shoulder. "Life isn't always fair." He handed Robert a dollar and went inside the cafeteria. Robert accepted the money like an entitlement, and Mary, gaping in stunned disbelief, felt a sudden twinge in her stomach: *Not only does he look like a bum,* she thought, *but smells like one, too. Why else would people be feeling sorry...?* That had to be it — the foul smell of rank, gut-wrenching odor. Only problem, there was none! Or was there? To be sure, she took in deep, robust breaths.

Her actions were most suspicious.

Robert removed his spectacles and blew on them, and wiped off the lenses. He put his glasses back on and furrowed his brow. "What're you doing?"

"Oh, nothing...!"

"Nothing...? You're sniffing around like a bloodhound on the hunt. What is it?"

"Nothing, nothing at all — except —"

"Except what...?"

"I've never seen anyone *give* you money before."

He shrugged his shoulders, and all was quiet.... He broke the silence: "It happens every now and again." He put the matter behind him. "At any rate —" he began.

Suddenly a stranger, yet another stranger appeared from out of nowhere. In his mid-forties and wearing a dark tailored suit, the man — frantic and out of breath — said: "Mister, have you seen Roxanne, my wife?"

"Why, no," said Robert. "As a matter of fact I don't even know your wife!"

"Then how do you know you haven't seen her?"

Robert fell silent, his face expressionless. Then, in a huff, he bellowed, "*WELL...!*" The man bugged out his eyes and dropped his jaw, and set off down the corridor. Robert turned to Mary. "So what night are you *free?*"

Again the "f" word was uttered, and Mary fell weak in the knees. "Free" in-and-of-itself wasn't bad...but "free" and Robert was a package deal — like beacon and eggs. Mary felt queasy every time he used it.

No matter the context.

"Why you ask, Robert? Wanna take me out on the town?" She softened her brown peepers, her eyelashes fluttering. She never expected a reaction, but react he did, his body shriveling and shrinking like a snow cone in Vegas.

She was beside herself.

"You know it!" said Robert, all but in a trance.

"You do; you really do?"

"I *do* what?" He shook his head, trying to kick start his brain back into motion.

"Want to take me out..."

"Why, yes — I mean, no!" he said, emerging out of his spell. "Did you forget? The team can't move ahead until you re-circuit the computers! There just isn't enough *time* in the day."

"Oh, I see," said Mary, though not convinced he wasn't hiding something. "Just name the day, Robert, and I'll be there."

"How does Thursday sound?"

"Thursday; got it...."

"We'll begin work at eighteen-hundred hours."

"Right, Thursday, eighteen-hundred...."

"Maybe afterwards we can grab a bite."

"'We'...?" As in you, me, and the whole rest of the team...?"

"C'mon Mary, you know what I mean. Just you and me..."

"But Robert, we've only known each other five years!" She threw him a smile, and Robert had forgotten — or had never fully appreciated — how beautiful she was.

"Five years?" He pondered, rubbing a hand up and down his chin, and Mary could never tell when he was being funny or serious. He said, "Five years, huh? Long enough! So how about it...?"

"It's a date!"

"I know this donut shop that makes the tastiest fritters. Have anything you want, anything at all. Sky's the limit! They even have a video game." He giggled...then added: "And tipping isn't required." He smiled, his mouth bracketing dimples — a smile that could evoke a spring day in the dead of winter.

Mary heaved a sigh and Robert was just getting over Betty Hudson, some girl he met at a rummage sale. It was awful, how after only one date he called on Betty for a second time. She no more than answered the door when Robert said: "Hi Betty...how'd you like to go out this weekend?" Her response was deadly. "I don't go out with many guys and I wouldn't go out with you!" She slammed the door and Robert froze solid, his spirits dampened. Moments later he bellowed, *"WELL!"*...and that was the end of Betty.... Not long after Betty came Amy Porter, a pretty girl from the secondhand store. After just one night out with Amy he called her on the phone, avoiding the slamming of doors. He said, "Hi Amy, this is Robert. Mind if I stop by this evening?" She said, "Oh sure, Robert, come on over...there's nobody home." Robert said, "Great...I'm on my way...!" And when he got there, there was *nobody* home.

The wife-seeker was again upon them. "Mister, have you seen Roxanne, my wife?"

"You, again...? You already asked me that, remember?"

"Oh, yeah...I'm sorry.... I don't mean to be a nuisance but —

well — Roxanne means so much to me. I don't know what I'd do without her." The man's eyes welled, and Robert remembered what it's like to lose someone dear. "Listen," said Robert, "can you describe her?"

"Why, yes! She's got a tattoo on her —" he began, his face going red. *"Skip that.* She has a birthmark on her —" The man got all flustered. "You can *skip that,* too." Mary felt ill-at-ease, and Robert, restless and irritable, tapped his foot impatiently. The man reached inside his breast pocket. "I've gotta picture of her, right here..."

"Now we're getting somewhere," said Robert.

He handed Robert the photo, and Robert perused it briefly. Mary copped a peak, and shuddered. Robert said, "This is your wife?"

"I know it's not a very good picture, but she's in her pajamas."

"Still, she's so...so..."

"Large, I know...very, very large...! *Jammies* aside, she's a knockout in a dress! Her dress size is a mere thirty-four inches...." The man's face fell. "She's a fifty-eight in pajamas." He let out a sigh. "But such is life"

Robert narrowed his eyes. "I see...Miss America by day, Miss Piggy by night. Now look here, it's *impossible* to go from a thirty-four to a fifty-eight in the span of one day!"

"She doesn't sleep with a girdle."

Robert turned to granite, his eyes blank. Mary bristled, fearing Robert might slip into *auto-think!* But didn't, and bounced right back. He turned to her. "How do I get into these things? He wheeled back to the man. "Don't worry about it. If she's clever enough to get out of her girdle she's clever enough to be found...! Just the same, hope you find *Roxie-poxie."*

"You mean, Roxanne."

"I feel I've really gotten to know her...! Now if you don't mind..."

The man turned and walked away when, not a moment later, a USAF Sergeant halted before Robert, peering into his eyes. "Excuse me sir...Mr. Meeks would like to see you in his office —

right away."

Robert jerked his head, clearing hair out of his eyes. He got all tense, his complexion changing colors faster than a set of Vegas strip lights. He felt cornered, trapped like a wounded lion. A large lump settled in the region of his Adam's apple, his voice shallow: "Thank you, Sergeant." He always knew this day was coming, but never really thought it would.

The sergeant set off down the corridor and Robert, his head throbbing, stared blankly into space. Mary looked into his blue eyes, realizing the twinkling light had gone out.

"You okay? What's wrong, Robert? Speak to me!"

Robert was on the precipice, his brain manufacturing images, his eyes seeing things. She studied him pityingly, all but expecting "auto-think": *Unintelligible ramblings, as though some psychotic stranger had stepped into his brain to use his mouth as a speakerphone....* But somehow it didn't happen. Not this time. Still, Robert wondered around in darkness, unable to discern the real from the phantasmagoric — a condition brought on by the dearly departed.

THE BILIONAIRE MISER WAS HYGIENIC, NOT AESTHETIC, HIS clothes stained, patched, and cost-saving. While waiting for the new hobo craze, Robert wasn't about to make a fashion statement! Still, his attire was clean and laundered, his mother strict about hygiene, training her son to wash both his body and clothes regularly. Obsessed with cleanliness, Robert was "automysophobic" — an abnormal fear of being dirty....

## Chapter 6
## THE WHISPERING SHADOW

THEIR JOB WAS SIMPLY TO ORGANIZE CRIME AND OUTFOX the authorities.

Nothing more!

At age 39, Raymond Frederick Moran was referred to as boss, his handle Moose. Boss Moose tipped the scales at 400 pounds, his height towering at six-feet-seven inches. He had a gruff voice, hair black and wavy, graying at the temples. His eyes were an intense green, constitution rugged. For all practical purposes Moose was the brains behind the Whispering Shadow — a byproduct of a criminal mind.

Horizon Tower was a hotel gem, nestled in Upper Manhattan. At 2:20 AM Horizon Tower was under invasion. The Whispering Shadow arrived through an unlocked balcony door, the gang heavily disguised, poised to elude the New York Police one more time. A redolence of mint filled the hallways, the hotel laden with marble floors and columns and polished statuary. The "Shadow" was a five man ring, two of whom were quite fat, inept, and *extremely* lucky: George Spence and Stanley Moran. While Stanley Moran was a balding "inept" with black hair, George Spence was a head enriched "inept" with flaming red hair. Still, Stanley knew more about "alarm systems" than most knew about "alarm clocks"…and George could handle anything from soup to nuts…a jack-of-all-trades. Apart from *consuming* everything from soup to nuts, they were both quite a standout — their big bellies standing way, way out. With that said, Moose Moran operated out of South Hampton, New York, and letting them go simply made no sense. As it were, Stanley was Moose's cousin, his first cousin…and while Stanley *outweighed* a baby elephant, Moose's sense of family *outweighed* his judgment. As for George — well — George was Stanley's best friend, and needed his buddy's support; he beseeched Cousin Moose to take George in. Moose threw caution to the wind and welcomed George into the fold…. George and Stanley were one and the same, inseparable as wine and roses — or in their case, milkshakes and pizzas. Apart from food, George and Stanley had *luckily* pulled down a lot of loose change, essentially getting by on luck — a remarkable run of luck. Moose was raking it in, and putting them out to pasture was not in the cards.

Security had just completed a walk-through, the hallways virtually void of people. The Whispering Shadow moved stealthily to the Presidential Suite, the air-cooled building helping to curtail sweating. Still, the heat was on, and their diving suites — worn beneath garments — *really* turned up the heat. It was all Stanley's idea, asserting that thermal-suits would deflect motion detectors, thereby throwing the security system's brain for a loop.

On bended knee, George jimmied the oak doors with a crowbar. Suddenly the doors sprang open and Moose, rushing in with a bound, led the charge. Time was of the essence, their specialty robbing the rich and leaving no trail.

Apart from George and Stanley, the Whispering Shadow offered three of the best — Moose Moran, Big Ed Malloy, and Cody Walker. In spite of George and Stanley, the NYPD thought they were dealing with an international gang of thieves. Instead, of five local bandits, two of whom were just lucky.

A shaft of light seeped in through the paneled curtains, and glimmered off *The General of Naples* — a 17th century oil painting over five feet high. The room showcased riches aplenty, their objective to haul away as much as possible. Other than traffic din from the boulevard below, the room was quiet, fruitful, and secure.

Just as it should be!

A clang rang out, prompting Cody Walker and Big Ed to draw guns. Moose flinched, as if smacked alongside the head; he whirled into his cousin for having *dropped* the tool bag. "What're you doing?"

"Sorry Boss, but that picture frightened the *heebie-jeebies* out of me...!" Stanley bent down to retrieve the bag.

"Are you crazy? It's only a painting!"

"It's the eyes...they're staring me down. They're alive!" Heads swerved into the painting, all but expecting the general to lash out at them. Still, the eyes stuck, glued to their every move, chilling them to the bone.

The general dropped *his* gaze to Moose, turning Moose pale white. He croaked, "Non —" He swallowed the second syllable, and tried again. "Nonsense...! Now don't make a sound!" They all froze, and listened for the beep — the security system's low beep. A moment later Moose went "Ah-ha!" He whirled about and dashed into the foyer, his men right behind — except George and Stanley, who were not *so* behind.... The panel was mounted on the wall beside a marble statue, and everyone huddled around it. Moose turned to Stanley. "Screwdriver, automatic...!"

Stanley reached inside the bag and whipped out the tool, handing it to Moose. Time was of the essence, and they had to feed in the correct "systems answer" or impending doom would follow.... The automatic tool whirled effortlessly around six metal screws, dropping into Moose's glove hand. Meanwhile, George studied *Neptune,* the upright sculpture next to him — it stood motionless, and was only just a statue.

Moose's pulse raced, like a surgeon on the verge of losing a patient. Stanley produced instruments calmly and quickly, and could well be an O.R. nurse.

"Quick, Security Code Bypass!" demanded Moose.

Stanley reached back inside the bag: "'Security Code Bypass' coming right up!" He pulled out a pair of broken binoculars and turned to George. "Here, hold this." George took possession of the separated tubes, wincing at the sustained damaged; the lenses barely held on, as if flattened by a hydraulic press. Stanley next whipped out bolt cutters, handing them to George. He then pulled out a crowbar, a hammer, a set of lock picks, and a *crushed* box of rubber gloves, all going to George.... Searching all around the bag, Stanley turned rigid, his face aghast.

"What...don't have it?" Moose locked his gaze on his cousin.

"Well, no...not exactly, Boss."

Stanley finally removed the Bypass, his fingers entwining wires, timers, diodes and switches, all one hairy mess.

"Fat ape — you sat on it!"

"No Boss, I didn't! Really I didn't!"

George turned to Moose. "Stanley sat on the bag all the way here, Boss. Fast asleep...!"

Stanley whirled into George. "You don't know what you're talking about — as usual!"

Stanley turned back to Moose. "Doesn't matter, Boss, I can bypass *it* manually."

"Bloated idiot — no time...! The alarm's going off any second. One little computer, that's all! When you gonna get it straight?"

From across the foyer, a slash of crimson had locked onto their thermal-offset, the seconds ticking down.

Stanley removed something from the bag — a *squashed* package. He extended the package to Moose, wincing in chagrin. "Twinkie...?"

Moose coiled with anger, his fingers contorting around Stanley's chins — Stanley had no neck — and proceeded to snuff the air out of him. *Saved by the bell,* when the earsplitting alarm suddenly rang out, prompting Moose to withdraw his hands and rocket out the door! Big Ed Malloy followed suit, as did Cody

Walker. George quickly shoved everything inside the bag and thundered into the corridor. Before leaving, Stanley whipped out a calling card, whirling it down to the floor. The card landed face up, the side in which bold letters proclaimed:
THE WHISPERING SHADOW....

THE ACCIDENT OCCURRED IN ROCKFORD, ILLINOIS, SHAKING Robert to the core. He was in Texas at the time, Johnson Space Center, Building 31, working on Thermal Vacuum Chamber A. Victor Map solemnly approached Robert, pulling him into a nearby conference room. Waiting inside the room was Lieutenant Becker, of Vehicular Homicide. The lieutenant grimly said: "I deeply regret having to tell you that your mother and father were killed while crossing the street."

Robert was an "only" child, and loved them dearly. The news was horrific, his heart stumbling over beats; his health took a turn for the worse. Upon discharge, he settled down in the area in which he was born and bred: the northern part of Rockford, Illinois.

His mansion rested on a 20-acre landscape, no expense spared.

Inside his Rockford home, Robert sat on an overstuffed recliner, the room cloaked in darkness. He just couldn't get the thought out of his head, the car flying by at 50 in a 25 zone, striking Bill and Lucille dead-on in the crosswalk. Too bad "Tony the Drunk" didn't include Robert, for he felt just as dead. It was like someone had ripped the heart clean out of him, leaving him no more animated than a cadaver. An event that ended two lives and three souls, leaving behind two corpses and one breathing creature who only wished he were dead....

"YOU HAVEN'T EVEN DONE MY LAUNDRY, NOW HAVE YOU?"

"But Mr. Smith, I did the laundry just yesterday," said Maxine Carter.

"Today's a new day, now isn't it?"

"All I asked was —"

"I *know* what you asked," said Robert, snapping at his

housemaid. "First you want to know why I live alone, and now this. You keep your long, pointy nose out of my affairs! You're nosey…just too nosey."

"What?"

"Oh, I'm sorry; not clear? NOO-SEEYYY! I fired what's-her-name for *less!*"

"Emma Franklin?"

"That's the one. She was nosey too. What I keep behind that door is nobody's business. Now pack your things and get out of here!"

"B-but Mr. Smith…"

"You heard me — out!"

Robert Joseph Smith, scientist turned browbeater, wasn't about to give an inch. Not with so much at stake.

The secret door was situated in the basement observatory, and Robert was quite sensitive to that which lay beyond. Anyone in violation of the "Mind Your Business" clause was fired on the spot.

The ol' heave-ho!

## Chapter 7
## THE LONELY RICH WIDOW

"RANDY'S CANDY IS O' SO DANDY" — A SLOGAN MADE IN heaven.

The candy wasn't so bad either!

At age 47, Jane Romero bagged Randy Hodges, a rich entrepreneur. Randy Hodges, CEO of Randy's Candies, ran a billion dollar industry; a giant among his peers. He met Jane at a party when he became infatuated with her, and she with him. In May of 1983 the couple eloped to Las Vegas for a quickie marriage…and life was good.

In 1998 they moved into their dream home, Hodges Castle, nestled in the rolling hills of Skokie, Illinois. The castle took after the middle-ages, and showcased wealth on every level. They had it all, including a rambunctious young niece named Ann. Great Niece Ann visited regularly, taking pleasure in the courtyard and moat; she too enjoyed the bastions, running up and down the spiral stairs yodeling and screaming, her voice echoing throughout. Ann also took pleasure in the medieval fort, replete with wax figures and weapons associated with the times. However, the dungeon and torture chamber was off limits to the little girl.

Ann was a living terror, prodding the "help" to skip and jump and rush in all directions; they invariably bumped into each other, knocking things over, Ann all wiggly and giggly. Of course, the little girl didn't mean to be mean and was just having fun. Still, Ann was the apple of her aunt's eye, and could do no wrong.

In May of 2014 Randy had become bedridden, stricken with congestive heart failure. Jane saw no point holding onto their 150-foot yacht and sold it. Randy Hodges died that same year, 2014, and island hopping in the Caribbean came to a screeching stop.

With hair of gold and vivid blue-gray eyes, Ann blossomed into a stunning beauty, seeing lots of men. One man in particular got under her aunt's skin: Mario "Sparkle" Forte…. Sparkle was Chicago's most notorious crime czar, and Jane was livid. While city officials knew nothing of Sparkle's mob ties, Jane knew all too well, outraged at the whole thing. She tried to discourage Ann from seeing him, but to no avail. Despite Jane's efforts, Ann and Sparkle got married, and Ann and Jane grew distant. To stay above the fray, Jane sought other friendships.

IT TOOK MORE THAN A "BILLIONAIRE'S CLUB" TO MEND lonely hearts.

Strait-laced Jane sat all alone in the cabin, on her way to Pet Adoption. With much on her plate, she ignored the flat-screen and poured yet another glass of the bubbly; she shut off the TV and, gazing out the window, enjoyed the ride, the limo moving easily through post-rush hour traffic. She hashed over seventy-six years of ups-and-downs, when her thoughts settled on the night before. She disregarded the car phone and buzzed down the Plexiglas partition, and studied Luther MacKenzie in the rearview mirror. "So tell me Mac, what are your thoughts on last night's dinner party?"

Luther MacKenzie raised his gaze to the mirror. "Frankly Madam, I wasn't invited."

Jane went cold, her fair skin ebbing under a blush of

embarrassment. "Rather, from a 'Valet' point of view."

The tuxedoed chauffer cocked an eye. "As a parking attendant, the running back and forth was great exercise. The side money wasn't bad either. No complaints."

Jane opened her mouth, froze, drew breath, and said nothing. The limousine turned onto Skokie Boulevard, the sun setting in the west, shadows stretching in the east. A cluster of storefronts blew past, and Jane, breathing heavily, was steeped in agitation.

"If you don't mind my saying, Madam Jane, you seem rather annoyed this evening. Anything you'd like to share?"

"I'm rehashing yesterday. Something about it makes *no* sense."

"What is it that puzzles you?"

"Oh...someone had made a comment and — well — just thought it was uncalled for. Got under my skin, you might say... So tell me, Mac, what *did* you think of Randy?"

"Randy and I got along really well; great guy."

"You're not just saying *that?*"

"No, my lady, I am not just saying that."

"Have you *ever* had past employer problems?"

"Frankly, yes..."

"Do tell."

"Young and inexperienced, I suppose. I mean, someone was always out to get you. Randy wasn't like that. True professional...a straight shooter...."

Jane released a sigh. "Thank you Mac; you've been quite helpful."

"Is that all, Madam? Sounds like something's missing from the puzzle..."

"Left out the best part, if you must know: Leonard Kazak. Everybody had wonderful things to say about Randy, except Leonard Kazak, CEO of *Choco-lite Delights.* Kazak had the unmitigated gall to accuse *Randy's Candies* of stepping on 'the little guy.'"

"What? Randy wouldn't step on an ant!"

"True, so true.... According to Kazak, Randy got ahead by

mere exploitation."

They stole glances at each other in the rearview mirror.

"Sounds like jealousy to me. How's his company doing?"

"Okay, I suppose. That is to say, for a meager 70 stores domestic." Jane drew up her nose, her face dripping with disdain.

"Did Randy really own two-thousand stores?"

"Randy left me an empire that spans around the globe. More like 21-hundred...not including the 76 stores currently under construction."

"Well now, there you have it — sounds like some unscrupulous rival jealous of your husband's success."

"Perhaps," said Jane, releasing a long and winded sigh. "I just don't appreciate the hypocrisy. Kazak was a rather good friend until last night, when suddenly he turned into a bloodsucker. Any common person knows that social events are for polite conversation and nurturing relationships. I am simply appalled at his blatant ignorance, his disregard to act in a controlled and civilized manner; particularly for one of his stature. However jealous Kazak may be it gives him no right to attack my late husband. What's more, that's the last dinner he will *ever* squeeze out of me!" Refilling her glass, Jane gave a quick but steady pull on the bubbly. Inside ten minutes she'd knocked down five glasses.

Following a brief but interesting exchange, MacKenzie drove to the pet store in complete silence. He thought about their conversation, wondering if he should offer a suggestion. *Best not get involved* ripped across his mind.

He simply went about his duties.

The evening had settled into dusk, the sun abating and fading, people hustling and bustling. The stretch limousine double parked in front of the pet store, when Luther MacKenzie climbed out to lend a hand to his employer. Jane Hodges was escorted out with elegance, stopping hoi polloi in their tracks, people gawking at the chauffeur's pomp and mannerism — at Jane's charm and sophistication. It happened suddenly, on the northwest corner of Skokie Boulevard and Oakton Avenue, where innocent people going about their lives were taken aback by Jane Hodges.

PET ADOPTION WAS ONE OF THREE PET STORES WITHIN THE city limits of Skokie. Owned by Brett Andrews, the store was practically stolen for pennies on the dollar at a bankruptcy auction. She'd since turned it around, supplying Skokie with all her pet needs.

Brett Andrews was in the backroom, inventorying her latest shipment of exotic animals. Meantime, hunter John Phillips waited inside the showroom, Pet Adoption his last run of the day; he needed Brett's signature before packing it in.

A wretched screech shot through the hunter's head, rattling his bones and knocking teeth loose. He turned, and saw a young woman squealing at the squirrel monkeys not eight feet away. The woman was short and stout, her mouth chomping crudely on dollops of gum — like a student of monkey etiquette.... Suddenly she latched onto the cage and started shaking it. All the while odor, a foul odor, fell off her person, stinking up the place. The cage shook with vigor, and the girl — peeved at how *less* offensive the monkeys than she — was in all likelihood jealous.... She infiltrated the bars with her fingers, the monkeys going about business as if overweight divas could do no wrong. This only intensified the young woman's efforts, prompting John Phillips to action. Making his way to Miss Obnoxious a sudden hush fell over the room. John turned, when something warm and fuzzy crept along his bones; he was taken aback by a vision of pomp and grandeur, his eyes going clear and sharp.

He rubbed his hands together, his powder-blue eyes twinkling like Hope diamonds.

Jane Hodges supported her arthritic body on a ferruled cane, hobbling across the hardwood floor with grace and charm; her gold-handled cane was a club of sorts, fending off lowlife when necessary....

John goggle-eyed Her Majesty's white and gold ensemble, which stole the show! Jane was looking her level best, her 150 caret necklace a cascade of light setting off that snowy neck of hers. John Phillips sensed a mystique, an aura behind the woman's apparel — her jewel encrusted tiara. John Phillips didn't have a moment to lose.

John Phillips had to act fast.

The old woman walked lamely around a man and woman gazing at a litter of puppies. She tersely said "Pardon me" and continued on, the cane leading the way; she verged upon the bird section.... Once there, she stood in awe at a plethora of birds vying for attention. The royal woman was drawn to the macaws, the largest birds on display; she wondered how big a challenge to teach a parrot to echo words. She studied the birds' powerful beaks, long tails, and brilliant plumage; the pros of owning a macaw tumbled through her head: *It may well be the highlight of my afternoon tea parties...the courtyard will be highly amused. The crumpets will taste most delightful!*

Something odd slithered in through Jane's nostrils, curdling her blood. Jane wrinkled her nose, hoping her flesh wouldn't crawl away. She turned, and Miss Piggy was standing right beside her. The stout woman was glued to the tiara — Jane's studded headdress. The 76-year-old sensed trouble, narrowing her eyes; she studied the young woman's crudeness, her acrid odor; the noisy gum chewing. Miss Piggy lowered her gaze to Jane's diamond necklace, inspecting the stones like a Marine officer inspecting troops. Jane sensed the woman's scorn, and braced for the contempt that generally followed. Like others she'd dealt with in the past, Her Regal-ness was poised to do it again.

"Are the bags under those eyes *Gucci?*"

"You shouldn't knock the rich, young lady; it's hard finding a job from a poor person."

"And what makes you think I'm not rich?"

Jane threw her nose up in the air. "Because, my dear, if you had *my* money you'd throwaway yours...!"

Irritated at the old woman's boost, Miss Piggy sneezed, when a wad of gum flew out of her mouth, landing squarely on Jane's upper chest, falling down her v-neck. Jane bristled, and promptly took her stick to the woman's head. "How dare you disrespect nobility?" But before striking, Jane choked, stifled at the law suits that generally followed; she backed off. She nevertheless bobbed her cane mere inches from the young woman's mug, saying, "I *could* let you have it right in the kisser but I see you've been punished enough there already."

Keyed-up patrons gathered round, and began a steady stream of murmuring....

The piggy woman flared her nostrils. "You're drunk, woman! Pie-eyed, completely smashed! If it wasn't for the olives in your martinis you'd starve to death!"

Strait-laced Jane lowered her stick. "I'll have you know, young lady, I prevail in a fortified medieval castle. What's more, as dedicated sponsors of royalty, my every whim is met hand and foot. I don't take gruff from any of my servants much less lowly commoners."

"I don't doubt you live in a castle, but what as, the court jester?"

Jane was exasperated. "Why, I never...!"

"What, 'never' wore the cap and bells and floppy shoes? No way...you're the funniest joker in the deck!"

Jane rang in the authorities, her eyes smoking. "Security, police, security, police...!" Big veins stood out on Jane's neck in cords.

"Pardon me, coming through, gangway," said the voice-of-the-people. John Phillips tore through like a dozen gangbusters rolled into one.

There was a time when safari hunting was fun and lucrative. Not any more. Nowadays it took a seasoned hunter to earn a descent living. John Phillips was just such a hunter. Still, he had issues, issues stemming from the Endangered Species Act. To date, the laws were stringent, the fines endless. Tired of the politics, John wanted out.... On a side note, John Phillips was still an eligible bachelor of 60.

John approached the two ladies, his manner unbiased. "Now what's this all about...?" Before Jane could utter a syllable the stout woman jumped in. "This old battle-ax called me a —"

"Tut-tut...that's quite enough, young lady." John gestured the woman in jewels with a single wave of his hand. "How dare you refer to this sweet, charming woman in a foul manner? Your conduct is despicable, young lady, very despicable!" He looked softly into Jane's eyes, those somewhat suspicious eyes. "How could you be so brash as to attack this lovely, sweet, adorable woman who stands before us like a dove, an innocent lamb?" John's voice quivered with emotion, sending tingles up and down Jane's spine. He swung into Miss Grotesque. "You should be ashamed, highly ashamed!" John turned back to Jane, focusing on her diamond and ruby tiara — her crown of jewels. John's eyes bulged like grapefruits, his mouth bobbing up and down but saying nothing. Suddenly he croaked: "Can't talk; my mouth...is...watering!" He turned to the crowd, and signaled the royal woman with a hand-wave. "Feast your eyes, ladies and gentlemen...hardly seems fair that Mother Nature should turn all this charm loose on unsuspecting manhood."

Jane rubbed her eyes, her vision all blurred: she saw the hunter's shirt morph into a gleaming breastplate, hands into leather gauntlets, his head a medieval helmet. John had turned into Jane's knight of armor!

John said, "Don't go anywhere; I'll be back. We need to talk, say...over dinner?"

Jane's heart froze, and barely nodded.

"We do have a date for dinner?"

"Yes, I should say so." Jane nodded affirmatively.

A broad smile split John's face. He swirled about and, latching onto the young woman's arm, sneered at the gawking faces before him. "What is this, a staring contest?" He barked loud and clear...like a Drill Sergeant: "Hay-yopp! Hoi-yahh-yahh-yahh-yahh...!" Everyone scattered about, running for their lives. John held firmly onto the young woman's arm and escorted her through the store; he led out the building. He quickly paid her off, and made her promise never to return.

## Chapter 8
## ROBERT THE ATHEIST

Lightning cracked overhead, rain pouring in every direction but up! It thundered and it roared, great drops beating on cars and rooftops, the wind howling like wolves in the wilderness; Gargoyle spouts gushed, water racing down sewers and inundating the city. Through it all Robert toiled in his vault, his underground vault, lined with greenbacks three layers deep, the shelves stacked solid. Hardly a wonder Wall Street should drop three points with vault deposits. Just the same, Robert plowed through piles of money, recording each and every serial number; his body ached, fingers stiff and numb. Like working the coffee fields, it was a grind: bill after endless bill....

Robert's home was situated in Rockford, Illinois, near the area in which he was raised. His property was well-groomed, graced in tall trees and fountains and polished statuary. The building itself was extensive, made of heavy-gauge steel and stone and solid concrete. The ceiling was high and vaulted, replete with sky-high pillars and lancet windows and artful stained glass. The building was dark and Gothic, resembling a 19<sup>th</sup> century cathedral.

Robert finally left the bathroom, his hands free of ink stains. He strolled towards the living room, and glanced up at the grandfather clock: 9:42 PM.... He continued on to the coffee table, and picked up the TV remote. He settled into his leather recliner and elevated his feet; got comfortable under a heavy quilt....

He yawned and stretched; money impressions were stuck in his head. He'd been gazing at C-notes for the longest time, and didn't scratch the surface. Exhausted, he decided to pickup the ledger some other time. He was also worn out from all those newspaper clippings — those countless coupons. Robert loved a bargain...swap-meet bargains in particular. In fact, he spent the whole morning there, the swap-meet, buying three pairs of jeans, two plaid shirts, and one hooded parka — relics from the 1980s. Plus three briefs and two boxers — the skid marks were hardly noticeable.

Robert punched the button, firing up the TV. He settled on a political commentary: *In Black-and-White the Left Is Right.* America was in dire straits and the show's host, Larry Parker, was buzzing from the "Kool-Aid." As it so happened, Democrats wanted to raise taxes, and Robert, worried they might tap into his pension, got hot under the collar. He muttered, "Taxes, yeah, right! Almost everyone's out of work and Parker wants higher taxes. Guess he didn't get the memo — taxes kill jobs!" Frustrated, he started yelling at the TV: "Hey Dems, how 'bout raising revenue through job creation! We don't need more taxes we need more *tax payers,* you stupid buffoon! He lowered his voice. "If Parker took idiot lessons he'd fail the test...!"

Still, after eight years of "Bush," Robert wasn't too fond of Republicans, either. *Combine both parties together,* he thought, *and what do we have: people eating like elephants and thinking like jackasses...!*

They broke for a commercial and Robert pressed Mute; he had that far-away stare, his thoughts gracing Mom and Dad — if only he could see them one more time. He lifted his horn-rimmed spectacles and rubbed his dewy eyes. The clock tolled ten, gong tones echoing throughout. Robert lowered his glasses, and began flipping channels; he needed something to ease the pain, his life a downward spiral — like driving at breakneck speed into a brick wall.

As a scientist, "afterlife" without proof was simply out of the question. Robert's faith was in the natural world, *not* in fairytales. Still, couldn't get over his loss, hoping something would prove him wrong. Of course, wasn't expecting fish to fall from the sky. Nor did he wish to be struck by lightning.

Just proof!

His face suddenly went bright. He muttered "Ah!" and stopped turning channels. He released Mute, and fixed his gaze to a group of experts examining the Shroud of Turin — *Millions of people believe the Shroud to be the actual burial cloth of Jesus Christ — an old piece of fabric with an affixed image of a crucified body.*

Robert listened with cautious optimism. The narrator said: "Several times the Bible refers to the burial linens of Christ. The shroud, believed by many to be *that* linen, was studied by a team of scientists to determine how the print of a body got on an old piece of cloth."

The cloth image was haunting, and Robert, wondering if it was Jesus' *actual* body, was unmoved, his eyes closing, head nodding. He dozed briefly, when his eyes shot wide open and gazed haphazardly at the TV. "In 1532," said the narrator, "the linen was almost destroyed one night during an accidental fire in a nearby church. Miraculously, the image itself was barely touched by the fire."

The program was interrupted by a commercial, and Robert, wandering back to his parents, paid little heed to the ad. He gawked at the screen and only thought of life and death.

Soon the program returned, and Robert, at odds with the presentation, was less than hopeful. The narrator said: "The first photo of the holy relic was taken in 1898, when the cloth image appeared as a photographic negative." Robert was somewhat stirred, but still not convinced. He rubbed his chin, and narrowed his eyes thoughtfully. "In this negative-like photo," said the host, "a wealth of details appears. The eyes are closed as in death, the body contours clear and distinct. Evidence of a wounded man, a man whose welts and scars matches Jesus' crucifixion in stunning detail. Still, the oddity here is *timeline,* as the image dates back five hundred years before the invention of photography...before anyone had seen or even imagined what a negative image would look like. Simply put, the Shroud had become more than a matter of faith but a matter of science." Robert sharpened his ears and became more interested. "In 1976," said the host, "a photo of the Shroud image was placed under a VP-8 Analyzer. Any two-dimensional picture placed under the VP-8 will appear distorted. But not the Shroud photograph. The Shroud photograph was transformed into a three-dimensional picture of a crucified man. In fact, no other photo will appear as the Shroud photograph: clear and vivid, every detail sharp. There are no other paintings, drawings, photos, prints or negatives in the world with such qualities. The Shroud image is the only one of its kind."

The goals of the team were to determine how the image was formed, and, what constituted the image. That is to say, whether it was paint or whether it was something else.... After more than 100 hours of painstaking research the team still didn't have a clue. They therefore cut out a piece of cloth for radio carbon dating, which placed the Shroud's origin some time between 1260 and 1390.

The narrator begged the question: "Since the Shroud was discovered in Lirey, France in 1352, is it possible for the Shroud to have been forged in France?" The Shroud was deemed a hoax. A medieval hoax! Robert sighed mightily. He said, "How could it be otherwise?"

Too bad the Shroud was like everything else in the Bible: fiction. Pure mythology! Still, Robert was rather pulling for *authenticity.* In light of the other, his parents were nothing but a twinkle in the eye of his memory.

He rubbed his teary eyes, resigned to the tragic *end.*

The program paused for a station break and Robert punched

Mute, reflecting on the cloth's image — burned, scorched, and seared into the fibers. Even more peculiar were the aspects of the image, appearing as a negative-like photo, and, three-dimensionally.... He raised a hand to the nape of his neck and rubbed. He said, "That *is* pretty strange...a two-dimensional object encoding a three-dimensional image!" Under his breath, muttered: "Such a forgery would be *impossible* to produce today much less eight hundred years ago...!" His hair haggard, clothes impoverished, he lowered the leg rest and sat up in his chair, and waited for the program to return. Once it had, he thumbed Mute-release, and watched as someone introduced a forensic expert. The man said: "The carbon dating is 'inconclusive' because of the fire of 1532. This fire parched the cloth, burned it in places, water was thrown on the cloth, thereby ruining various parts of it. The cloth was subsequently repaired — a repair that took place in the middle-ages. While forensics didn't know it then — nineteen-eighty-eight, when a piece was cut out for testing — they know it now. That is to say, the textile used to mend the Shroud in the middle-ages was that which was tested in 1988. The medieval portion of the cloth, in other words, was *inadvertently* tested, producing a bogus origin — between 1260 and 1390. Unbeknownst to the investigative team, the tested material — not the original Shroud — changed the carbon dating by *many* centuries.... The discovery was amazing, utterly astounding, giving credence to Christianity and rocking atheism to its core."

Though his skepticism was waning, Robert still wasn't convinced. Something *had* to place the Shroud in the Middle East if things were to become interesting.... Little did he know that that was next, because soon a botanist explained: "Thirteen microscopic pollens were lifted from the Shroud, pollens native only to ancient Palestine...plants still growing in Israel and *not* in Europe."

That was just the beginning, as the pros kept coming and Robert's jaw kept dropping. "Christian art shows nail wounds in the hands of Christ," said the narrator. "The Shroud, however, indicates blood spurting from the wrists."

He saw a pathologist experiment with cadavers, driving nails in through the palms and hammering the bodies onto wood beams, hanging them upright. Surprisingly, the flesh would *not* support the weight, and tore away. Then, as illustrated on the Shroud, nails were driven in through the wrists. Here, the tendons and ligaments could easily support the weight. The Shroud image was accurate.

Still, forensics couldn't explain away the image.

The program, not yet over, introduced a radiologist. The man explained how that radiation, when channeled through the body, will create a detailed human image. "By way of Medicine Imagery," said the expert, "I was able to duplicate on film the image on the cloth; that is to say, three-dimensional qualities as that of the Shroud. How ever incredible the cloth that I worked with — fresh out of the photo lab if you will — couldn't hold a candle to the 2000-year-old Shroud in terms of sharpness. Somehow the Shroud image is strikingly more vivid. I don't know what instrument was used to radiate Christ's body," said the man, "but the technology was *far* superior to 21<sup>st</sup> century man."

Robert figured if radiation had created Jesus' image, then Jesus' body must have turned to light, imprinting His image. He pondered: *Could this mean Jesus conquered life through resurrection?* The back of Robert's neck prickled. With a glassy stare and mouth wide open, he proclaimed: "Jesus truly *is* Christ!"

Thanks to the presentation, Bill and Lucille's prospects for existence were quite good. Resigned to immortality, Robert opened his closed mind and vowed to take everything he'd learned since age one, every scientific strategy ever applied, every second of training received from NASA and search out his parents. His "deceased" parents! For what appeared to be the tragic *end* would now mark the beginning of a new chapter.

## Chapter 9
## THE SHADOW RETURNS


W HILE THE INTERNET KEPT COMPUTER HOUNDS ABREAST
and advised the "newspaper" remained the center of information.
The *New York Viewer* was favored among the general reading
public, its circulation up. The building was headquartered in
Manhattan — a granite and stone high-rise on Roosevelt and 42$^{nd}$
Street, southwest of the East River. The paper covered news 24 /
7…and nor was it flawless, occasionally getting it wrong.
Supporters, however, overlooked such details, buying in record
numbers….

The wee hours continued into the night, the New York
Borough glittering in the skyline, the Viewer billowing in the
waters below.

Larry Higgins sat attentive at the information desk. Moments
later he raised his gaze to the familiar shoe clicks, the rover
heading his way. The rover, Bruce Mahoney, was a burly man
with razor-thin mustache and wire-rim glasses, his uniform khaki
and dark brown, shoes high gloss.

Mahoney stopped at the desk at precisely 2:59 AM. "Go on

break, I've got it from here."

Larry Higgins nodded and rose from his chair, and made for the cafeteria…. Mahoney no more than signed in when five distinguished but unusual looking men appeared from shadow. All five had smug expressions, their opinions of themselves favorable, including the incurable air of importance associated with people of the underworld. George and Stanley appeared a tad broader than usual; they sported dark sunglasses and classic press cameras, which hung around their stubby necks. Big Ed carried a black duffel bag. Everyone wore black overcoats and fedora hats and fake goatees; their hairpieces and noses were a diverse mix, and Hollywood could not have done better.

Sportswriter Michael Dorgan was recently rolled. Big Ed needed Dorgan's Press Card, just his Press Identification Card. Ed was an expert counterfeiter who, with an enormous frame and shifty brown eyes, could produce highly crafted documents all of which were absolutely official-looking and absolutely phony.

In tight-lipped silence they handed the guard fake press cards. Mahoney glanced at their mug shots and unwittingly copied bogus numbers in the journal. He gave them back their identification and handed Moose the clipboard. Moose signed-in and — without appearance of undo haste — they set off across the floor, three-of-five gliding…two others trudging.

Everyone but Cody headed for the elevators; Cody veered towards the marble steps, on his way to Video Surveillance, his job to take down the guard and render the video equipment dysfunctional.

Weighing in at 136, Cody Walker used to train at Clyde's Gym in The Bronx. He started boxing at a young age, his highlight an impressive win record for the Amateur Boxing League. His trainer, Jack Hill, begged him to go professional but Moose Moran had made a better offer.

George and Stanley tossed Ed their cameras, and Moose thumbed the elevator button. Ed shoved the cameras into the bag and the metal doors slid open; they all climbed in.

The elevator rose smoothly to the seventh floor, and pinged

softly. The doors slid opened and Moose, stepping casually into the corridor, took in the area, his gang right behind. The coast was clear, which came as no surprise, it being the wee hours.

They moseyed down the hall when George suddenly got cramps; he toddled up to Moose, his bowels inflamed. Moose turned his head without breaking stride. George had that stunned look about him. "Gotta go, Boss…bad, really bad…!"

Moose ground to a stop, his face tight with anger. "Get real! This is no time to take a —"

"But Boss?" George interrupted. "I really, *really* gotta go!"

"Go, just go! And be fast!"

George ran laboriously down the hall for the Men's Room.

STANLEY STOOD WATCH AT THE PAYROLL DIVISION DOOR, the door ajar. He craned his neck into the lighted hallway, the room behind dark. His frame massive, Stanley sported a felt hat, dark sunglasses, classic goatee, and fake nose — on the lookout for suspicious-looking characters.

Meanwhile, Moose and Ed worked on the safe, the diamond drill punching holes and weakening the tumblers. Everything was going as planned — the door well guarded; cameras dysfunctional; the safe no longer safe.

George suddenly appeared from out of nowhere, waddling hastily to payroll; Stanley reveled in George's efforts to get to work and make good, a crooked smile creasing his face. But as George came into view Stanley saw utter shock, as if his buddy had done it in his pants. Stanley drew in his head, and George, pushing through the doorway, was frantic and out of breath. "You're not gonna believe this." He spoke in short, shallow gasps.

"What?"

"Place is swarmin' with cops!"

"Cops…?" Stanley's blood ran cold.

"*Coppers* everywhere, like some kinda *Fuzz* convention! They're onto us — jig's up!"

Stanley turned to stone, wondering how things could get any worse, the a.m. hours just settling in after yet another long and fruitless day. Now this...! His face lopsided, Stanley yelled down to Moose. "Cops...! *Fuzz* everywhere!"

A second later Moose yelled back: "Quick, everybody out of the building!"

Before barreling out the door Stanley pulled out a calling card, tossing it down to the floor: **THE WHISPERING SHADOW**. Next, with the precision of two ballerinas, George and Stanley took to their heels, whirling smack dab into the doorframe, getting stuck back to back. They wiggled and jiggled when Stanley finally said, "You're blocking the doorway! Get out of the doorway!"

"Gimme a break, would you? Can't you see I'm stuck?" Their bellies pressing into the frame, George said, "Relax, just relax! We'll let out all the air, okay?" George waited for a response but none was forthcoming. "You hear what I said?"

"I heard, I heard! Just do it!"

"On three... One...two —"

Suddenly Moose rocketed around a cubicle, flailing his arms and shouting: "Out of the way! Out of the way, I said!" He cradled his elbow and plowed into them, catapulting them into the hallway. Moose spilled onto the Payroll Division floor, moaning softly; Ed extended him a hand, hauling him back onto his feet.

The Whispering Shadow — minus Cody Walker — jetted blindly into hallways that ran left, right, and straight ahead, looking for the nearest flight of stairs. Big Ed led the pack, and was first to spot the stairwell EXIT. He ran up to the door and, before pushing through it, urged on his cohorts. When they caught up, they thundered into the stairwell and flew down the stairs, two at a time — George and Stanley one at a time. They huffed and they puffed, the stairwell shaking like Jell-O on a buzz saw.... Upon reaching the first floor, they all collapsed under a fire hose in the semidarkness; they panted breathlessly, their blood pumping, hearts pounding.

Minutes later they ambled through the lobby, like just another day at the office. They encountered no police, just one guard dozing at the information desk. They straight-armed the glass doors and exited the building, leaving Cody Walker behind.

* * *

THE ALLEYWAY WAS COLD AND DARK, FOUR MEN lingering outside two black Cadillacs.... A high fence half-circled the Viewer, the alleyway lined with garage walls and warehouses, a smattering of garbage-cans throughout. The post-midnight moon hid behind clouds, a redolence of fish and river water wafting, low fog rolling.

Moose strode back and forth, hoping Cody would make it out safe. Stanley, meantime, was a complete wreck — a seesaw of *ups* and *downs:* last week "down" for having damaged the Security Code Bypass; this week "up" for having sounded the alarm.

Moose should be thanking him.

An October chill clung to the fog, the alleyway dark and quiet.

A twittering sound cut through the silence. Moose stopped pacing and removed his cell phone, picking up a call.... "Who is this?"

"Whassup?" asked Cody.

"Why aren't you down here with the rest of us...?" As Moose heard Cody out, Stanley could only imagine what Cody was telling him. Moments later, Moose roared: "No, job's off! Place is swarming with cops! Hurry, get out...!"

Stanley sighed, relieved that *that* was *that.* But when Moose failed to terminate the call, Stanley shuddered. Especially when he heard Moose say: "Stanley, that's who! I got it from Stanley. Now hurry and get out! Police everywhere...they're infiltrating the building!"

Another time-lapse, and Stanley sank to a new low, shriveling and shrinking like a punctured old tire. He thought, *If only I could dissolve into the fog.*

"Janitors...? Did I read you right...?" Brief delay.... "Uh-huh...I see. No police, just janitors," said Moose, echoing Cody's words.

Moose squared his shoulders and, without ending the call, tossed his phone to Big Ed. "Here, take this."

Ed raised the phone to his ear, his foot resting on a metal can.

"Doesn't look good, Cody…Moose is turning green before my eyes — dark green. Looks like a ripe avocado with ears."

EARLIER, UPON SUBDUING THE GUARD IN VIDEO Surveillance, Cody departed for Payroll when, ambling down the North Hall, heard strange noises from around the corner. He stopped cold, and crept up to the intersecting corridor; he peered down the hallway, and saw a battery of policemen and policewomen, all adorned in navy blue and wide black belts. His eyes grew wide, his jaw thudding against the floor. But then — not a moment later — realized they were all milling about, waiting for the gear locker to open up….

The NYPD was the cleaning staff.

Janitors in blue!

Cody shrugged it off, and continued on to Payroll.

*KLICKITY-KLAP — KA-BOOM, ZONK, ZAP!*

Cody Walker stood among a network of cubicles, his cell phone pinned to his ear; he cringed at all the strange and foreign sounds emanating.

He heard a peace offering, a "Twinkie," when *bam!* a metal garbage can came crashing over the phone, as if falling down an elevator shaft. Moose bore down on his cousin like Godzilla to an elephant, using Stanley for practice.

All the while Cody's ear twisted and twanged, his hearing all but impaired.

## Chapter 10
### SPARKLE THE MAGNIFICENT

THE STAGE WAS SET, DRAPED IN BUNTING AND STREAMERS and oversized balloons, all poised to rain down at the opportune moment.

Mario Forte stood alongside the mayor, the room opulent and formal. The mayor took the spotlight, his hand signaling Sparkle, the man by his side. He spoke into the microphone, his voice resonating: "Rosemont would like to offer heartfelt thanks to Mario Forte for the common good of our villagers. First, his efforts to protect the health of our economy, and not least the health of our environment! On behalf of the citizens of Rosemont, it is my pleasure in presenting Mario the Key to the City, a token of our esteem and affection...."

Mayor Jack Sullivan lowered his gaze to the head table, his dearest of friends, all of whom looked fondly up at Jack. It was a two-thousand dollar a plate dinner, and seemed that every money-minded dignitary from the city was here: "here" being The Sparkle Resort and Country Club. Sparkle, whose real name was

Mario Forte, had an uncanny knack for drawing crowds. The reason for the dinner — well — wasn't important. Any motto, any slogan, any gimmick would suffice. The huge banner said it all:

IN APPRECIATION TO<br>
MARIO FORTE<br>
FOR<br>
HELPING PROTECT THE ENVIRONMENT

Mario Forte accepted the Key with humility, which wasn't easy for someone adorning a sequin tux and jewel encrusted cape; most especially, for someone with two huge statues of himself erected on either side of the stage.

The clandestine czar was an award magnet, and the Village of Rosemont knew nothing of the man behind the mask. To his boys, Mario Forte was a man of superhuman strength whose life was dedicated to the good fortune of evildoers. To his fans he was the cornerstone of integrity, whose generosity was unequalled for the sick and needy — a superstar of breathtaking apparel and bloodcurdling excitement.

In all appearances Mario had gotten the award for discharge flow protectors, which prevented power boat contaminates from spewing into Lake Sparkle. In truth, the award was for all the bribes, or contributions pouring into various political campaigns. Still, there were too many ins and outs, too many temptations…too many greased palms. With that said, the mayor rather enjoyed the common "flashbulb"…particularly when flashbulbs popped and approval ratings soared. Politicians would bask in the glow of TV lights, talking at never-ending length to well-groomed on-the-spot reporters, patting Mario heartily on the back and shaking his hand, smiling broadly into news-cams.

One hand washed the other and everything was aboveboard.

So it seemed.

SIX YEARS AGO, MARIO RAN AN ILLICIT GAMING establishment in Lake Forest, Illinois. His activities were strictly hush-hush, no one any the wiser. All the while city officials were preoccupied with red ink, the economy sluggish and slow. Mario didn't skip a beat, kissing-up and gaining favor; he prodded the mayor — plus The Honorable Mr. John T. Miller (governor) — to lobby for a land base casino. The idea was to generate money into Rosemont, and "Sparkle" — an alias describing Mario's love of precious stones — would be just the one to pull it off. As expected, the land base casino was approved and State Regulators granted Sparkle his gaming license....

The groundbreaking event took place in the Village of Rosemont, northeast of O'Hare International. It went off without a hitch on the first day of September, 2009. Sparkle received a trophy, a plaque, and Lucite bauble shaped like the Coliseum in Rome. He said a few choice words, cut the ribbon, and twenty 14K gold shovels drove into the dirt.

The Sparkle Resort and Country Club opened almost three years to the day — the 27th day of August, 2012. They had live music, fireworks, balloons, and free hotdogs. The resort highlighted a clubhouse, which was detached from the forty-story hotel / casino. The lake, Lake Sparkle, had a marina w / observation deck, and boats of all kinds. The golf-course was aesthetic, 36-holes of rolling greens and intermittent curtains of water. The hotel replicated the Coliseum in Rome, and thus named The Roman Empire. Mario remembered the first time he stepped inside the gaming area, his very own "legalized" casino. He all but stopped breathing, taking in his remarkable achievement: hand painted frescos depicted gladiatorial combat, chariot races, and Roman soldiers slaying wild beasts. The high-rise building had two HD dance clubs and a slew of lounges...marble columns, Florentine statuary, and Venetian chandeliers throughout. In keeping with the Roman theme, the structure was elliptically shaped, reminiscent to "The Coliseum." An array of high-end shops encompassed the casino, giving a boost to the Rosemont economy. Everything for which Sparkle had been striving had finally been attained.

On a side note, the hotel was so big it had restaurants on the way to "the restaurant."

THE SHORT-IN-STATURE ICON HAD STRENGTH EQUALED TO Godzilla's....

His hair was jet-black, cropped short and glistening with gel. He had hazel, clear as diamonds eyes; the set of his jaw imbued him with a wrath worthy of a king. At 34, Sparkle exercised regularly, a physique attained *not* by performance enhancers but rigorous gut-wrenching workouts. He was a picture of health, a testament of someone who never smoked and never did drugs — he rarely drank and consumed plenty of fruits and vegetables. His complexion was bronze, which shimmied like polished brass in the sunlight. His teeth were bleached, whitened to brilliance. At $7 thousand an ounce, personalized cologne mirrored his high-strung, savvy, and quick-to-take-offense personality.

EXERCISE STARTED EARLY, WHEN THE FIRST ROSY PINKS OF dawn nosed over the horizon. The courtyard was his workout area, where a concrete pool and never ending gardens and vista cafés graced the site. A view of the harbor rested beyond, where high-powered boats and acrobat skiers entertained guests from late spring to mid-fall. With that said, Sparkle preferred crack-of-dawn workouts, when most guests were fast asleep in their soft beds, away from the courtyard and away from he.

Following routine warm-ups Sparkle transitioned into a cross-resort run, trotting past tennis courts and setting off across Sparkle Fairway. He ran along a ridge laced in shrubbery and greens, working his mind as well as his body. He tapped into his Psychic Reception Area, and engaged in a common Western progression — I, III, VI, II, V, I. While random numbers and puzzles were equally effective, he chose something to which he could relate — the science of music.... Having completed the series in all sharp and flat keys, he rotated the Greek modes around the Circle of Fifths. Of course, it wasn't like he needed the music lesson; Sparkle could recite this stuff in his sleep. He was merely shifting his awareness upwards, to the crown of his head, stimulating his alpha-brain-waves — something he'd learned from Shi Shan Yong, his kung fu instructor. Shi Shan Yong was a Shaolin Monk, an Eastern philosopher adept in the art of telepathy; abilities obtained at a temple in Northern China. Thanks to Shi Shan Yong, Sparkle — through "heightened" awareness — could tune into any location at any time, all inside his head.

He ran on the roadside which paralleled the lake, sweating and panting and feeling fine. All the while his third eye surveyed the grounds, looking into various areas. He peered inside the casino, and saw a wee gathering — indicative to the wee hours.

Business as usual....

The image faded into another: the clubhouse lobby. In his head he saw Mr. G (high-roller) sprawled out on the sofa, reading the paper.... The stretch of his legs felt wonderful, the rhythmic slap of polyurethanes under the rising sun of a glorious fall sky. His balanced joggers gave a spring to his step, almost making him weightless.

Sudden dread fell over him. He stopped dead in his tracks, his mind imaging activity outside the boathouse not a half mile up the road. He gave the matter a quick study and resumed his run, deviating from his normal route.

THE WOOD BURNING FIRE PITS SAT OPPOSITE THE boathouse, the U.S. banner furrowing in the wind.

While the front of the boathouse appeared peaceful and calm, the *back* of the boathouse wasn't quite so, as nine angry warriors bided their time, waiting patiently for Sparkle.

Each warrior wore a mix of ethnic dress and modern combat garb, all capable of speaking English — to a degree. Orders were to incapacitate the man of bronze. Not kill him, just cripple him.

A warrior wandered to the front of the boathouse, the area overlooking the flagpole. He inadvertently raised his gaze to the lake when the corner of his eye caught someone creeping in stealth. The warrior drew breath, and pointed a digit at the creeper. "Sparky nigh, Sparky nigh...!"

The remaining eight warriors barreled to the front, crying a bloodcurdling chant. They converged on Sparkle as Sparkle converged onto them, all leaping over the flagpole hedges.

Sparkle arrived at the flagpole at a full sprint; he grabbed the pole as his axis and swung his legs around, slamming his jogger into a man in his line of fire. The warrior catapulted into the man behind, the two falling senseless down to the ground, out like lights. In one fluid motion Sparkle elbowed a man in the ribs, throwing a savage punch under another man's chin.

A trained fighter pivoted 340-degrees, aiming his foot at Sparkle's head in a mind-blowing spin. Sparkle's peripheral glimpsed the foot projectile, throwing up his arm to block the incoming kick. Startled at Sparkle's swiftness, the man's mouth fell and his eyes blinked.

Sparkle leapt into the air, smashing his head into the face of a man hovering over him; he rammed a fist into the man's solar plexus, sending the air out of his lungs like a squeezed accordion. The man fell dazed and bewildered, out cold.

Fang Shao — Master of Deception — had had enough.

Fang Shao removed four cylindrical canisters from his billowing garb, flicking the levers to each, tossing them close to Sparkle. The cylindroids hatched bluish-looking smoke that rose to a thick, cloudy haze, consuming all visibility.

Grunts and groans and the dull thud of blows emerged out of the smoke, when someone tried to escape the suspended carbon. Suddenly an arm flashed into view, yanking the man back inside.

Sparkle was fully in the moment, ignoring the smoke while letting instincts deeper than thought guide his every move. Stronger and swifter than the rest, Sparkle leapt and punched and kicked and blocked, ignoring everything except the opponent in front of him.

Once the smoke wafted, nine warriors lay moaning on the cold, damp ground.

Sparkle lowered his gaze to the wasted bodies, and snorted in contempt. Suddenly three grandmasters appeared from out of nowhere, stopping before the man of bronze. Their heads hooded, the grandmasters were all cloaked in flowing white habits, all relatively similar one from the other: prominent bones, muscular, distinguished noses and chins, faces highly resolute.

Sparkle shuffled closer, his demeanor humbled.

"You are remarkably skilled, my Sicilian warrior," said Shi Shan Yong, Grandmaster of Kung Fu, bowing in reverence.

"So well-versed in the fighting arts," said Aviv Imi Sarao, krav-maga instructor, lowering his head.

"Your agility and strength is admirable," said Kulin King, Grandmaster of Muay Thai Boxing, his body bending forward.

Sparkle spoke meekly: "My abilities are but a reflection of discipline and training, which I humbly attribute to my mentors." He lowered his head. "I shall value it always... Please, spend time here at the resort...a few days. A week! My home is your home. I will call upon my house doctor to attend the ailing, these fine warriors selected to test my skills." Sparkle gestured the defeated with but a single wave of his hand. "The concierge will arrange your rooms and plan your dining. Should you need transportation chauffeured limousines shall be at your beck and call."

SPARKLE'S TRADEMARK WAS STYLE, HIS ATTIRE FIRST-RATE. He had a fascination for things that sparkled, explaining away hoards of sequin tuxes. The fur coats and capes, however, were imitation, as Ann advocated the ethical treatment of animals. Mario's wife simply wouldn't allow the *real deal,* thus supporting the senseless slaughter of animals whose only crime was to bear fur.

To keep peace, Mario capitulated, and wore imitation.

Like the late pianist, *Liberace* — who dazzled audiences around the globe with stone studded attire — Mario *too* played the piano, and, was quite good. His boys in fact likened Mario to *Liberace,* coining the *nom de guerre* "Sparkle." Incidentally, all his piano keyboards were *not* of ivory tusks; rather, the vegetable ivory — a hard substance obtained from the ivory nut.

## Chapter 11
## ON THE HUNT

JANE HODGES NEEDED THAT PERFECT COMPAMION, THAT perfect friend, someone, anyone, to replace Randy's love and affection. Only problem was age. Jane was past her prime, and finding a mate wasn't easy. She simply settled on a pet...a bird with the gift of voice.

But wound up with John Phillips instead.

She put John up in a hotel, and arranged his transportation — a stretch limousine shuttled John to and fro the castle daily. Meantime, as it so happened, the 60-year-old hunter was an avid storyteller, charming Jane's guests.

THE GREAT HALL WAS DONE UP IN MEDIEVAL FASHION, THE affair opulent and formal. The castle was festive, comprising of doctors, bankers, and entrepreneurs. It was a sizable bash, a carnival of dancing and chamber music, the food endless.

Adorned in black tie and tails, John Phillips looked pretty good for one approaching the golden years. His wardrobe consisted of tuxes, suites, and accessories, all bought and paid for by Jane Hodges, who merely saw it as an investment...and was usually right about her investments.

John stood before a two hundred-plus audience, poised to deliver a true-life saga. He studied the faces before him, his body well-defined, powder-blue eyes still sharp.... He spoke calmly into the microphone: "I'll never forget my first hunting experience. I was in India, and the sign read: 'Fine for Hunting.' The hunting was *indeed* fine. I bagged my first tiger and then I paid the fine." Laughter broke out, and Jane barely cracked a smile.... John cleared his throat, and continued. "One night in Africa, I decided to stake myself out. I spent all night in a small tree over the carcass of a zebra, attempting to lure a lion out into the open. There I was, alone and vulnerable, when it finally happened."

His timing was perfect, especially when he held out his hands as if to answer questions...but being a man of great importance he just didn't have the time.

John lowered his gaze to Martha Higgins, an attorney's wife; she sat on edge, trying to refrain from nail biting. Martha Higgins surveyed the area, waiting for her moment. The second no one was watching she swooped up a carafe and filled her deep basin goblet with wine.

"Suddenly, and without warning," said John, "I, the hunter, had become the hunted!"

John dramatized his words with the flair of a seasoned stage actor — wiggling his fingers, flailing his arms, shouting at all the right moments. "Instead of stalking the bait, the lion had instead stalked me!" On cue, the audience let out a convulsive gasp.

John's telling wasn't for the faint of heart, as Martha Higgins' complexion had gone white over her frail, squeamish body. Her condition was that of a blood trauma, and fainting was generally the norm.... She whisked up her goblet and guzzled greedily, as if dying of thirst.

"For two hours the lion slowly crept around and around the tree I was in. It edged nearer and nearer, threatening to spring up the mere 12-feet that separated me from the ground. Horrified, I took aim, and fired two rounds." All at once the audience went *Ahhhh...!* Cold chills ran up and down Martha's spine, and drank more liquid drug. "It went down," said John, "and a second later got up, coming at me in its crippled condition!"

The audience went *Ooooh!* and Martha slipped into a psychosomatic escape, blacking out. Screams collectively rang out, the timing flawless, creating the perfect sound effect. Doctors everywhere rushed to the woman's aid, suspense looming over John's predicament.

"The animal lunged up from the safety of my perch," said John, "when I got off yet another round. But the lion just threw out its paws and roared ferociously, and kept lunging. The most I could hope for was a lucky shot. All the while my rifle trembled and my heart pounded my nerves raw. I was never more scared. Then suddenly, to my relief, it ran off into the brush only to be found dead the next day — 30-yards from where I had shot it."

The Great Hall was lifted by John's words, moving the assembly to ovation. They chanted: "En-core, en-core..."

Jane sat with arms folded, her face smug. She raised her gaze to John, who just grinned at her. "You look charming tonight," he said.... She threw back her light stole and the famous diamonds round her snowy neck flashed. John added: "Those stones become you so."

Jane peered through her jeweled opera glasses, her eyes squinting, burning a hole through John.

WHILE TURNING IT INTO A LOVE AFFAIR WAS IN JOHN'S BEST interest, he didn't want it to be obvious. He therefore placed the ball in Jane's court, leaving it up to Jane — not he — to make that suggestive first move.

It was quite enough to strive for acceptance much less openly "dig gold."

John really poured it on, his demeanor refined and courtly, feeding into Jane's self-esteem. She was most flattered, graced by the hunter's distinguished mannerisms. Particularly when he tipped his hat and kissed her hand, like her Randy used to do....

John never asked for money or favors of any kind, keeping it professional. As a show of gratitude, Jane picked up all out-of-pocket expenses; such as lodgings, rations and travel. She even paid for four of his buddies who, on hiatus from India, swung by for a short visit — a three week visit. Like a blank check, all John did was sign and Jane paid the entire tab.

She often wondered what might happen if, say, John were to move in with her. The only problem was friendship. John was too good a friend to risk uncovering a different facade, a shocking new persona behind the charming John Phillips.

To risk losing...!

She played it safe, and paid for his stay out in town.

It was like yesterday when John Phillips sweated buckets in the sweltering grasslands. The next, riding up the social ladder of success. Not only was he a good friend, he was her escort — Jane's exclusive escort. But hey, nothing about it was demeaning. John lived high, and the road to fortune was just too alluring.

He went the distance.

The opulent couple was chauffeured to and fro art auctions, charity balls, and societal affairs. They attended Broadway hits and matinees, and ate the finest fare at the finest restaurants. They flew to London just to hobnob with the rich and famous. There, they saw Salisbury Cathedral in Wiltshire, one of the most cherished landmarks in the nation. They visited Durham Cathedral, where one of the earliest examples of quadripartite vaulting climbed high up the walls, walls arcaded in interlacing arches.

They saw Windsor Castle *and* Conway Castle in Wells; they barely had time enough to attend the memorial services of Warner Lenox — former chairman of *Contour Diamonds,* who had died at the age of 93.

FROM LONDON TO NEW YORK — TO QUINCY'S AUCTION House in New York City, where "bargain shopping" simply didn't exist. All Jane bought were a couple of paintings: a Van Gogh, and Monet. The tab came to $32 million and John, thinking he'd lost his entire inheritance, collapsed in a chair.

He got up to look for *Sugar Mommy,* scanning the area like a wolf on a sheep farm; he browsed through several of the galleries, appearing to be an avid art lover.

He spotted her in the central hall, inspecting Egyptian mummies and scarabs and the like. He walked casually in her vicinity, stopping diagonally behind her back: "Psst! Yoo-hoo…!" She turned, and saw John wink, beckoning her; he lured her across the hall, into the Michelangelo Gallery. John had that way about him…a certain twinkle that suggested haste.

Jane walked haltingly but nimbly on her cane, passing the Statue of David; she made her way into an alcove near the Roman god of wine, Bacchus. She looked perplexed, wondering what this was all about. John could barely talk. "B-b-but Jane, thirty-two million is just too much!"

"No, it's not. Not really. Besides, it's all relative."

John's face fell, his mouth parched, throat scratchy.

"What you don't understand, John is that the rich buy high-ticket items not because *they* appreciate in value but because *they* can. Furthermore, spending money is good therapy. It alleviates stress."

"Stress…?" John's eyes welled, his heart pounding somewhere in the region of his Adam's apple, his Adam's apple cider. "You know Jane, I've been under a lot of tension lately and, I was just wondering if you'd be so kind as to give me say, oooh…ninety, a hundred million dollars…"

Jane threw up her cane, as if to bop him with it, when a pair of glasses shot out of the handle; she stared John down through the lenses.

John pressed on: "You know…sort of as a gift. A hundred million really isn't much — it's all relative. Why, one-hundred million means nothing to you — peanuts, a mere bag of shells! I mean, if spending money relieves stress, think about it, a hundred million dollars will take years off my life…and you'll feel good about yourself!"

Jane didn't flinch and she refused to blink…. She lowered her cane. "Yes, John, indeed…spending money does wonders, therapeutic wonders. However, you'll have to get over it. If I gave away *that* kind of money it'd land me on my death bed. What's more, being the shrewd woman operator that I am, I wouldn't give you a hundred cents. Unless, of course, those hundred *cents* were certain to yield return! So you see, John, much as I'd like to I can't. I simply can't." She tightened her steely eyes. "By the way…I already feel good about myself. But nice try…." She flashed a crooked smile that was both confident and scary.

John shuttered, his heart slamming against his chest, his cheeks flashing pink. He just never expected this. In retrospect, however, he did nothing wrong commenting about the paintings, the $32 million. But it should have stopped there. Because now that his sickness, his "greedivitis," was in the open, Jane couldn't help but be suspicious and weary — a steady weariness brought on by age and the constant pressure of safeguarding her wealth.

JOHN TRIED TO CARRY ON BUT THE FEELING WAS GONE…AS were his desires. Still, John wasn't a quitter and, frankly, neither was Jane. They both clung to their interests, determined to succeed regardless of the odds against it. It was the aggravation, is all. So disappointing!

So frustrating….

Not long after, things started to pickup, their relationship back on the mend, clicking like a castanet — John smiling, Jane frowning.

*Just like before.*

Then suddenly, without warning, trouble fell out of a clear blue sky. It all began one cold night, one cold and frosty night when John somehow saw into the future…like "Scrooge" and the *Christmas Ghost….*

John saw himself as one of "them"!

It was horrible, just horrible.

The month was January, a Friday, the night cold and dark, icy wind shimmying John's bedroom window, waking him out of a deep slumber. He laid flat on his back, and slowly looked out the far corner of his eyes without moving his head. An eerie silence hung in the room, and John felt a presence — eyes watching him, looming over him. He sweated coldly, and looked around in confusion, and saw nothing; he thought it was all in his head, and relaxed his vigilance.

With a sudden urge to disembowel, John rose, and headed for the bathroom.

But rather than go to the bathroom he veered to the closet — he blindly walked into his closet. John was in a trance, his direction skewed, utterly distorted. His bathroom duties would just have to wait, for John was under the command of a higher authority — the specter hovering over him just earlier. It was pulling him, forcing him against his will, his thoughts a torrent. Images flashed before him, and John knew he had to give up something of himself for a higher cause. Confused, he headed straight for his tuxedos, trudging past hunting hats and Zambia vests and rhino hide pants.

John had to don a tuxedo before going anywhere or doing anything.

It was a chilling experience.

John couldn't take a *dump* without his tux!

HE GAVE IT HIS ALL AND COULD DO NO MORE.

Rather than go back to the drawing board, he stopped chasing rainbows and faced the music. Taking stock, John realized he was doomed, domed to his tux 24 / 7…! Fed up, he decided to go back to his livelihood. He had to get away from the high-muck-a-mucks, the captains of industry, the presidents and their conglomerates — their social clubs, their billions.

The snootiness!

Keeping "poshitis" in check, John got a yellow fever booster and renewed his passport. He booked a flight to Kenya, Africa, and couldn't leave fast enough. But leaving on a sour note wasn't good. John had too much invested, and leaving in a bad way would prove irresponsible. He therefore devised a plan, a plan that targeted the "will." Making inheritance his priority, John schemed and plotted like never before.

Going to Pet Adoption, he bought the most colorful parrot.

## Chapter 12
## NO DOGS ALLOWED

ROBERT SMITH ENJOYED SOLITUDE, HIS HOME HUGE AND
Gothic, like something out of the Dark Ages. The interior was
lofty and majestic, décor stylish, elegant in every way. The
basement, however, was paneled in stainless steel and rather
mundane. Essentially, the basement was a research laboratory,
bustling with high-tech doodads and cool gadgets and enough
blinking lights to send off to Mars. Adjacent to the lab was the
observatory, where a retractable dome accessed a 40-inch
refracting telescope.

Robert owned a comb. However, combs were *passé,* his head
chaotic and entangled, hair all over the place. Somehow his
vagabond attire lay beneath a perfectly tailored, immaculately
clean, and superbly pressed lab coat.

Go figure.

He yawned and stretched, his eyes burning with tiredness. To
stay focused, he cross-referenced data, rechecking his figures.
When he was through, made for the Smart Board, weaving through

a maze of obstacles.... Once there, he set his gaze on the board. He muttered: "Via the pineal gland — our third-eye — brain cells are in direct contact with the cosmos. Unlike sensory neurons — which transmits information to the brain — the pineal gland is the seat of the soul, transmitting information *outside* the brain. In essence, the pineal gland is that which determines destiny — soul destiny — by way of angelic / demonic nucleus centers...a network of space-time passages stretching across the universe. Since both worlds — heaven and hell — are connected, both struggle to affect soul outcome, linking the brain to its appropriate nucleus center in ways the internet links the computer. That being said, the amino group in cosmic dust is 'that' link!" Robert yawned and stretched, and needed a *pick-me-up.*

Steering clear of floor cables, he set off for the kitchen, just past the high-power laser.

He ambled into the kitchen and, ignoring the vending machines, approached the sink. He filled a bowl up with water, and placed it inside the microwave; he set the timer. Reaching up, he opened a cupboard and retrieved a cocoa packet. His mind clouded, read the directions: "*'EMPTY CONTENTS* into hot water and stir...'" The microwave "beeped" and Robert removed the bowl, pouring hot water it into his NASA mug. He tore open the packet, all the while *half-life* isotopes and "empty contents" joggling his head. Stationary $d/s$ 100 and "empty contents" too joggled his head, as did sphere 5D and axis $T$-matrix." His mind well joggled, he "emptied the contents" — into the wastebasket...! He stirred aimlessly, and muttered, "Once isotopes of biotic carbon are duly sequenced, a stew of nitrates will cultivate." He placed an elbow on the stainless steel counter and posted his chin in a cupped hand...cleared his throat, scratched his cheek, and sipped. His eyes turned squinty. "Taste weak!" He lowered his gaze to the steamy water. *"Hmm...must be defective!"* He examined the brand name: *Hot and Chocolaty...!* He retorted: "Never again!" and put away the packet for later. He clenched his teeth. "THEY JUST BETTER REFUND MY MONEY!"

With mug in hand, he strolled back into the lab. His mind

distracted, muttered: "Once a given particle reaches mass x two, a negatively charged messoooo —" Robert lost his footing, hurling down to the floor in a mad flurry of arms and legs. It happened suddenly, his jogger clipping a cable. He went "down" faster than a bad day on Wall Street...as if standing on top of the world, where extreme gravity draws into the Earth's center. All the while water splashed, the incident laying him flat, his glasses sitting cockeyed on the tip of his nose, his hair up, down, and all around. His lab coat soaked, he leaned up on elbows and snarled at the bolted down cables. "Oh well...such is life." He hauled himself up and straightened out his glasses. "The hot-chocolate lost its punch anyways."

He treaded past the multi-wave oscillator and set off for the workbench. When he got there his cell phone rang. He took the call. "How may I help you?"

"Hello, Mr. Smith...Mike Hardy here."

"Mike Hardy?"

"You know, 'Thrifty Groceries'! You wanted me to call before picking up my tip."

"Tip...?" Robert swallowed dryly.

"You know; my gratuity. You said to start a running tab, and you'd pay one dollar per trip."

"I said *that?* Me? *Moi?*

"Yes; don't you remember?"

"And did you start a running tab?"

"Of course...!" Mike heaved a sigh. "I know it's not much, but I could sure use six dollars."

"But Mike, you made only five trips. I owe you five dollars!"

"Oh no, Mr. Smith, I made *six* trips."

"How do you know you made six trips?"

"Because my records say so...! Besides, I weigh one hundred-and-fifty pounds...."

"You weigh one hundred-and-fifty pounds? What's that got to do with it?

"I started out at a *hundred and sixty-two* pounds...and every time I go to your house I lose two pounds. And since I weigh one hundred-and-fifty, I lost twelve pounds, which means you owe me six —"

"I know, I know! Look, on your next delivery I'll put you on the scale and pay accordingly...how's that...?"

"Sure thing Mr. Smith.... See you on Wednesday. Bye-bye!"

The call ended, and Robert punched Contacts; he scrolled down to the Greek Kitchen and hit SEND. A man answered. "How may I help you?"

"Placing an order for delivery..."

"And what would you like?"

"I'd like one chicken gyro with fries...a Greek salad with extra olives, and a Coke."

"Will that be all?"

"That will be all. May I have the total?"

"Just a moment.... That comes to twenty-two dollars and ninety-three cents."

"Very good..."

"What is your name?"

"Smith... Robert Smith."

The voice turned harsh. "'Gothic mansion' Robert Smith...? 'Upper North Side' Robert Smith...? 'Atwood Forest' Robert Smith...? 'Three-seventy Old River Road' Robert Smith...? *That* Robert Smith...?"

"Why, yes!"

The voice turned even harsher. "What are you doing about those dogs?"

"Dogs...? What dogs? I have no dogs. I'm allergic to the furry beasts."

"Foam curdling dogs are running my people off your property! What're you doing about it?"

"My dear sir, dogs do *not* dwell on *my* land. I have *no* dogs! I sneeze and break out in a rash with dogs. You *must* be getting me mixed up with somebody else. Are you going to deliver my food or are you not?"

"We'll deliver, but make sure those dogs are locked up."

"I tell you I got *no* dogs! If dogs are running people off my property they're somebody else's! They're *not* mine!"

"Fine...we'll be there in thirty minutes!"

"Fine...I'll be waiting."

Robert no more than hung-up the phone when the back door slammed, echoing inside the lab. He raised his gaze to the self-closing doors, which parted, admitting the help into view.

Groundskeeper Earl Dexter slogged across the floor with Grace Hunt by his side; they stopped before their *frugal-mister*. Grace Hunt, age 34, wore a sturdy black maids dress and apron, her carrot-top a web of ringlets and curls.

Robert turned to Grace, his eyes penetrating. "Did you do my laundry like I had asked?"

"But Mr. Smith, I scrubbed *all* the floors and vacuumed all the carpets. Washed *all* the windows, inside and out! Did the marketing, darned five socks, stitched three pairs of pants and patched four shirts. No time. Besides, I did the laundry just yesterday."

Robert shook his head, his tongue clicking: *tsk, tsk.* "Frankly, Grace, the details of your laziness do not interest me.... I want it done everyday."

Grace split a frown. "As you wish, Mr. Smith, as you wish...."

Earl Dexter — a brown-haired man in his mid-forties and wearing dirty gray coveralls — braced for interrogation. Robert said, "How's the pruning coming along?"

"Mission accomplished, sir, all the gardens, all the shrubs and all the trees — ripped, clipped, snipped and stripped bare to the bone. Not a problem. The problem is the statuary."

"Statuary...? What seems to be the problem?"

"Wax, sir, wax is the problem. I'm all out of it."

"But you *had* twenty-four cans!"

"Twenty-four cans weren't enough, sir — barely enough to buff and simonize six statues. Regrettably, Mr. Smith, Marie Antoinette ate up the last can."

"She did, eh? How many more cans?"

"Oh...thirty oughta do it."

"Thirty? Thirty more cans?" Robert froze, his face going blank; he shook his head, trying to clear it. "Fine, you got it. I'll look for a coupon… By the way…did you look at the car?"

"Yes sir, I did. The problem is the fan belt."

"Fan belt…? What about the fan belt?"

"You're wearing it."

"Oh…so I am! Look, just buy a new fan belt and I'll pay you later. Incidentally, the kitchen is stocked, fully stocked. Relax…unwind. Go eat something…I insist. You'll feel better."

Grace pouted. "Gee Mr. Smith, thanks a bunch."

Earl brooded, his face glum. "If I had any brains I'd quit this job!"

"What was *that* you said?"

"Did I say it? I was only thinking it…."

THE PICTURE WINDOW WAS A MARK OF ELEGANCE, adorned in Belgium lace and silk overlays. Robert stretched out on his overstuffed recliner, his legs elevated, covered in a heavy quilt. The room was cloaked in darkness, as Robert inadvertently gazed at the TV; a blank screen. Apart from a howling fireplace brought about by the wind outside the room was quiet and meticulously clean, thanks to the efforts of Grace Hunt.

Robert wondered if he'd have to pay for his food. He sighed, and mused: *Stranger things have happened.* His wandering mind lighted upon Earl and Grace — their pouting faces. He muttered, "Such swell workers, too. Just what will it take to cheer them up? Maybe if I gave 'em more money…" His shoulders drew up in a shrug. "Nah... Why should I be the one with the sour puss? Better *they* should be unhappy than me!"

He giggled.

Robert shut his eyes, and fell fast asleep.

THE GRAY VW TURNED INTO A WIDE DRIVEWAY, THE driveway lined with tall trees and untrimmed hedges. The car came to a sudden stop, cut off at the gate. A speaker box sat on the driver's side, where tall trees, tall grass, and chocking brush sat all around. James Finch peered through the trees, looking for the house…but couldn't see past. He punched the code outlined on the speaker box, and spoke into it: "Hel-lo…Mr. Smith…can you hear me?" James got no response. He shrugged his shoulders, and surveyed the area; he realized he had to hoof it on foot. He'd simply have to pick and claw his way through the forest.

OFF IN SLUMBER LAND, ROBERT DREAMED OF BEAUTIFUL Mary Evans…. Suddenly his eyes shot open, his head going icy-numb, barking dogs rattling his nerves and knocking his teeth loose. He flew out of the recliner and bounded into the foyer, and leaned into the peephole; he hit the porch light, unlocked the door, and stepped out onto the porch. His eyes swept the area, and saw four rabid dogs retreating into the forest. In the dim light, spotted a maroon heat-wave bag sitting out on the grass! He meandered down the stairs, and walked casually across the lawns, veering towards the bag. Once there, stooped to pick it up. He twisted his eyes. "What on earth is *this* doing here? Ah…must be dinner. How do you like that? Didn't even have the courtesy to ring the bell! I suppose he wants a tip. Really…?" He let out a spate of guffaws, turned, and retraced his steps back up the stairs. Going inside, he moseyed into the dining room; he lifted the Velcro flap and removed his food. "Guess I'll put the bag in the closet with all the others."

He let out a high-pitched giggle.

SECURITY HAD TOP PRIORITY, THE DOGS NOTHING SHORT OF a hologram! The system was *high-fi,* producing 6,000 watts of concrete sound. A laser beam, photographic plate, mirror, and PIR sensors sat atop two flatbed dollies, set to tracks. Via roller chains and sprockets, the flatbeds would move briskly out from either side of the forest and "V" into the front stairs. All the while dogs would lash out, terrorizing any and all life in its path.

GRACE HUNT AND EARL DEXTER ENGAGED IN CHIT-CHAT; they sipped hot coffee, the basement kitchen well-stocked.

"…His lab coat proves my point," said Grace.

"Doesn't prove a thing," said Earl, point-blank.

"Sure it does!"

Earl rubbed a hand up and down his neck, and pondered....
"No, it doesn't. Really, it doesn't!"

"Still not convinced, huh? Then how 'bout the Nobel, when
Smith got the Nobel…?"

"What about it?"

Grace lifted her cup, and sipped.... "Smith's mug was
plastered all over the TV and internet. I suppose you didn't see it?"

"No, I didn't. So what of it…?"

"Wore a stunning three-piece, hair well-groomed, tie perfect
— sharp as a tack...." She set down her cup. "Doesn't *always*
dress like bum."

"Can't see him wearing anything nice…just *can't*. Biggest
tightwad on the planet.... Doesn't add up...."

"Does…"

"Huh?"

"Worked for this guy once, Milford Franklin — filthy rich.
Just as cheap as Smith...."

"Impossible!"

"He owned a beautiful estate, ten expensive cars, and dressed
like an indigent."

"Indigent?" said Earl, raising a brow.

"A bum…pauper — vagabond!"

"Ah, like Smith! Go on, I'm listening…"

"The parents turned Milford into a miser. Sure, they provided
all his 'needs,' but never any wants *or* desires. Not even an
allowance!"

"What are you saying…?"

"I'm saying that 'need' means everything to people like that.
It's an obsession. Whenever 'need' is in the picture, everything
must be top-of-the-line — the best."

"'Yeah — well — maybe.... It still doesn't explain away his
lab coat. His perfect lab coat...."

Grace shook her head. "You're not getting it... It's

psychological. Smith yearns for 'need.'"

"'Need'...?"

"Right, 'need'...! His home is a 'need,' hence The Ritz-Carlton. Whenever he feels that special 'need,' sky's the limit — the best of everything! His lab coat is a 'need,' hence neat and clean.... If Smith, say, were invited to a social gathering of some type, he'd be his usual sloppy self."

"Oh, like always...!"

"On the other hand, if the affair were related to science, *voilà*, he'd be royalty.

"You know, I think you're on to something..."

Grace rubbed her hands together. "Just the same, nice of him to restock the kitchen for us"

"Wasn't it though," said Earl. "'Go eat some food,' he says, 'I insist! You'll feel better...!' Think I'll take him up on his unselfish offer."

Earl rose, and moseyed over to the vending machines, and inserted his money.

## Chapter 13
### CASH TALKS

Hodges' CASTLE LAY DEEP IN THE VILLAGE OF SKOKIE, Illinois, where medieval wonders never ceased! The building was made of concrete and stone, all mortared together. Clean water ran through the structure, and electricity facilitated all amenities. Hodges Castle was sprawling and majestic, replicating Chillingham Castle in England. Like 17$^{th}$ century Chillingham, Hodges' Castle had a torture chamber, battlements, and moat. The only thing missing were the frights, as Chillingham of England was said to be haunted — strange feelings of being watched and shivers of ghostly spirits prompting unexplained goose bumps to run up and down spines.

So far, no such happenings at Hodges' Castle....

So far!

*Pleasant dreams....*

A round table dominated the room, the bedchamber large enough to house three whole families. Madam Jane sat calmly at the table, her face expressionless; she sipped tea, and discussed matters of interest…. "You don't have to explain, John. Think nothing of it. Surprising you held on *this* long. Can I offer you a spot of tea?"

"No thanks. I'm fine…really."

The royal woman propped her royal chin onto her royal hand, and yawned. Disinterest radiated from Jane's visage, taking the news of his leaving rather well. John frowned at her demeanor, her casual concern: her soft eyes, her peaceful voice, the inordinate calm. She had this far away look, of the type an autistic person might possess.

John quickly modified his plans. "Of course, I won't be away indefinitely. I'll be back in a month or two, and when I do, you and I will paint this town red!"

"Hmm…now there's a thought." She rubbed her delicate chin, and could care less.

John cocked an eye. "You're not yourself, Jane. Is something the matter?"

"Why, no John. What could be the matter?"

"Don't know…" John drew his shoulders up in a shrug. "Just that everything about you seems…subdued."

"Subdued?" She smiled a little, and then emptied her expression. "I'm training myself to disregard pain. I think Stoicism is apropos."

"Stoicism…?"

"You know…indifference to pleasure and pain. And now that I have a parrot — a living, breathing creature to echo my words — I'm feeling quite indifferent, particularly towards pain."

He furrowed his brow and tried to make sense of it — the parrot echoing her words. But John had much on his plate and gave it no mind. His only concern, really, was the will — Jane's last wishes. Still, the problem was demeanor, as Jane's demeanor was off-kilter, and John couldn't put his finger on it: her quiet voice, the peace within. She wasn't normally like that, and John feared it might affect the inheritance.

She leaned sideways in her chair, and settled her gaze behind John's back; her face danced and glowed with interest. John turned around in his seat, and pinned his eyes to the blue and red macaw — his going away present. The bird stood nobly on the perch, like an eagle; its head was turned sideways, so as to fix an eye on the royal woman. A silvery light emanated from the bird's giant eye, almost washing away John's guilt for planning to leave high and dry.

"Please, John, don't take my manner the wrong way. I'm just glad you thought of me. You made me *so* happy. Because until now, until you brought me this lovely parrot I just didn't know *what* to do! I simply didn't know how to handle it."

"Handle it? Handle what?"

"Something personal… Something *long* overdue…"

John's breathing stopped dead in his lungs. "Personal?"

"Oh, no John, nothing to do with you… Well…maybe a little. But it's not bad. I just can't say what."

"Oh…I see. Then *hey,* if it suites your fancy, have at it!"

John truly didn't care what Jane was up to so long as the parrot pleased her. After all, the parrot was *his* gift, no one else's. A gift guaranteed to credit, to reward him at some later time. And if she *were* planning something, better still, as it would give her something to do, something to shoot for while he was away.

John swiveled his gaze to the masonry wall above the stone hearth (fireplace). An oil painting hung on the wall. The painting was a likeness of Jane. It depicted her in a formal Aristocratic dress, the neckline moving below the shoulder, the ruff falling into a gauzy kerchief. The gown displayed a full slashed sleeve with a rosette ribbon on the upper arm…then finishing off with a laced cuff at the wrist. Jane appeared highly resolute, her cheeks rosy, chin jutting, lips pursed, eyes balls of fire — she could well pass for Queen Elizabeth I.

"WITH RESPECT, MADAM, THE HOUSEHOLD STAFF IS talking," said Bryce Grayson, chief butler. "They would like for you to get out more…like you used to."

"Would they, now?"

"I don't mean to be blunt, my lady, but the crew thinks you're heading towards a breakdown. They say it's not healthy talking to a bird all day and all night. In all likelihood, they say, you could be teaching *it* the Gettysburg address! It's got me worried, madam...their mutterings are borderline mutinous."

Seated at the round table, Jane Hodges gazed imperiously up at Bryce. She hit the Stop button on the player when the parrot froze, and fixed an eye on the tuxedoed butler. "And why are they talking when they *should* be working?" Bryce looked down at his feet, as though his high-gloss shoes had suddenly become interesting. The arrogant woman pursed her lips. "Tell me, Bryce, do you think the help would stop whining if, say, I took away their benefits, canceled their furloughs, and revoked all privileges?" The butler slowly raised his head, his sheepish eyes gazing through his steel-rimmed glasses. He offered no response.

"Well now...that just *might* be the answer." Her tone was menacing.

A steady stream of unease trickled through the butler's veins, his eyes swimming from behind the spectacles.

"Come, come, Bryce...I've known you for the better part of fifteen years. You've always been loyal — staunch, true-blue. I trust you will tell those people to mind their business. Furthermore, if I find dirt in this building, anything out of place or out of line — anything at all — I will discharge both the Detail Supervisor and subordinate responsible. No excuses, no bellyaching, no second chances. They're fired!"

The butler fell dim. "Will that be all, madam?"

"That will be all."

Bryce turned, and proceeded to the door, his gait uneven and defeated. The parrot shot up all frenzied-like: "Don't do it; you'll be cursed for life!"

"Now, now Cash...let's not be rude," said Jane, regarding the bird.

JANE HODGES NEVER BORE CHILDREN, HER MATERNAL instincts nourished through Great Niece Ann — the daughter she never had. Nothing was too good for Ann. Jane therefore established a trust, a twenty million dollar living trust, to be paid on or after Ann's eighteenth birthday.

Following high school, Ann got engaged to Mario "Sparkle" Forte. Not yet married, Sparkle came to Ann for her trust fund, the principle — all $20 mil. He needed $20 million, plus $60 million of his own for a down payment on his lavish resort and country club. Ann complied, withdrawing the money from her account. Jane was shocked, outraged, as if she'd been robbed! She confronted her niece when Ann explained away Sparkle's money woes; however, not to worry, as Sparkle would pay it all back. Of course, Jane wasn't buying it, declaring Sparkle a parasitic leech.

The wedding was happy and nice and full of spice.

Things didn't sour until after the honeymoon. It was uncanny, as though Jane Hodges — or even the parrot, for that matter — had put a spell them…. If *only* Ann had listened to her aunt…! Still, the *spell* worked like a charm: As Sparkle fretted over *earnings* Ann fretted over *boredom,* the resort turning her into a grape, withering on the vine from inattention. But what could her husband do? Everything was riding on his enterprise. Even while the resort opened to big profits Sparkle was floundering, struggling to deposit $300 thousand in Ann's individual account each and every month. Still, Jane could care less, disappointed at the whole thing.

Ann had no problem with the mob.

The problem was business meetings instead of vacations, phone calls instead of quiet dinners, gifts instead of love. It frightened her at first but now it was more boring than frightening. What she really needed was friends; Ann was gregarious, and longed for acceptance. To stave off boredom, she made it a point to see Great Aunt Jane at her every convenience.

JANE'S WORK WAS FINALLY COMPLETED, THE BIRD coached and primed, ready to tell all! She was especially elated to see Ann, kicking up her heels and painting the town red. John Phillips too dropped in, the three of them dining at the world's premier restaurants — the finest efforts of the finest chefs. They attended symphonies, off-Broadway hits, auctions, and charity balls. Jane, John and Ann really hit it off, every day a new adventure, every night a hot time.

John returned from safari regularly, when it all came to a screeching stop in March of 2015...when Jane Hodges received a fatal blow from Angel of Hope Hospital.

The hospital finally started to settle down after yet another day of judging the sick, the sicker...the sickest! While the nurses' station outside Radiology was peaceful and calm, Radiology itself wasn't so calm.... Dr. Jonathon Massy sat at his desk, studying Jane's chart.... He reached for the phone, and dialed the number.

Jane picked up just after the sixth ring. "Hello!"

"Hello Jane...Dr. Massy here."

"Hi, doc...so what's the verdict?" Jane's voice was raspy and hoarse.

"I need you to stop by the office to go over the biopsy results."

"Sorry, no can do...feeling under the weather. Just give it to me straight and over the phone."

"Well, okay, if you insist.... The prognosis is bleak." Dr. Massy looked up and over his glasses at the computer screen. "The tumor is malignant, and spreading."

The news stung Jane into silence.

"Jane, you with me...? Hear what I said? It's spreading!"

"What are my options?"

"Not many, I'm afraid...medication and chemotherapy. That's about it."

Jane shuddered, her life flashing before her.... *"Chemo...?* I wonder if I read you right." Before Massy could respond a guttural voice, from Jane's end, rushed over the phone: "Don't do it; you'll be cursed for life!"

Jane heaved a raspy sigh. "I just decided...no *chemo.* "

"But Jane, chemotherapy is a viable alternative. Whoever said it isn't?"

"A little *birdie* told me."

"What?" Dr. Massy wrenched his face.

"I just don't want it, okay? No *chemo!*"

"Well then, I suggest you appoint a Medical Power of Attorney."

"Who do I have? I've got nobody."

"What about your hunter friend, John Phillips?"

"No dice, John's in Africa."

"Then how about your niece, Ann Forte...?"

"Yes, well...I suppose. Guess I have no choice."

"Incidentally, the wife and I are planning a couple days at the resort, your niece's resort..."

"It's *not* my niece's resort," roared Jane. "It's Sparkle's!"

"Oh, I see.... Just the same, you must be mighty proud of him. What a guy, huh...?"

"Who...? Proud of whom...?"

"Sparkle, who else...? I mean, what with *all* that money he raises for charity..."

Jane turned livid, her blood pressure off the chart.

The doctor continued: "Anyone who solicits for the sick and needy with such enthusiasm *can't* be all bad. There just aren't enough like him. Truly a model citizen, a pillar in the community, a really outstanding — "

"Shut it!"

"Huh?"

"Enough already!" barked Jane. "What're you trying to do, kill me? Is that it? 'Cause if that's your aim let me tell you something ...I've already got two feet in the grave so don't trouble yourself!"

JANE HODGES SAW IT COMING, TEACHING THE BIRD ITS lines. Now, one year later, "Cash" — named after an old flame — was dying to tell all. Having pondered her great wealth, Jane had decided to give nearly all of it to charity. Only but a fraction was to go to Ann and John: Her plan was to route money without Mario ever knowing it. And the parrot was just the thing to pull it off.

Shortly before her death, Jane cleared all 30 housekeepers off the property, from 2:00 to 5:00 PM. All that remained were two sentries at the gate. At precisely 3:03 that afternoon an armored truck rolled past the gate. It drove through and about the gentle rolling hills, up to and over the drawbridge, clearing the gateway; the truck motored around the courtyard and taxied to a stop at the main door.

Engine running, the truck's rear doors flung open when five armed guards unloaded a fairly large Anvil case. The custom made case was set on caster wheels, thus requiring only one guard to haul it through the Great Hall. Four guards formed a cordon around the case, all heading for the library. Once inside the library, Jane instructed where to place it. The heavy-duty case held 1000 straps, each strap containing five-hundred $100 bills — $50 million in all: $25 million for Ann, $25 for John. Since Jane had to out-fox Sparkle she had told no one; not even her entrusted attorney.

No one, except her beloved parrot — Cash!

## Chapter 14
### SPARKLE THE MUSICIAN

THE VILLAGE OF ROSEMONT TOOK PLEASURE IN THE Sparkle Resort and Country Club. Most notably, the jobs created. Thanks to the land based casino, Rosemont was back on the map and Sparkle was the *bomb* — the greatest thing since sliced bread.

The corruption was a whole other matter.

The Grand Salon was situated inside the clubhouse, where fingers danced across a full concert grand. By age nine, Sparkle had committed *Prelude in C# Minor* to memory. Now 34, he facilitated the keys like a pro — the *rallentandos,* the *accelerandos,* and *arpeggios* masterfully under his fingers. Playing the piano vented stress, and Sparkle was under a lot of stress. His problems began six years ago, when his best friend — Moose Moran — played thief-in-the-night, ripping him off.

Apart from settling an old score, Sparkle wasn't about to play professionally...not with so many starving musicians at hand.

Racketeering was the way to go.

\* \* \*

"THE MARRIAGE THAT STARTED OUT WITH A BANG QUICKLY whimpered, collapsing like a house of cards.

Once cherished by Jane Hodges, the parrot was now under the direct care of Ann Forte…and Sparkle was losing his mind.

If only he could get rid of it.

Ann knew her husband's sentiments, and felt betrayed. She had to confront him. "You hate Cash! Just admit it!"

"No, No! I love animals! Your parrot hates me!"

"Hates you, yeah, right…! I don't think so. I saw what you did, shooing it out the window!"

"I was swatting flies. And besides, it came back, didn't it?"

"With no help from you…!"

"Not my fault your parrot flew away."

"You leave my Cash alone or you won't hear the end of it!"

They argued over everything. They even argued over where the bird should stay, Sparkle insisting it stay in hotel storage while Ann insisted on *their* room, their luxury suite. But Sparkle would have none of it, and settled on the room next door: a suite allocated for ambassadors, senators, and statesmen — the rich and the famous.

RAMÓN BANDERA WAS BORN INTO A LOVING HAITIAN home, on Chicago's Northwest Side…. Ramón Bandera had a yearning to be a physician since boyhood, carrying out his ambitions in high school; he got in four years pre-med and graduated in the top percentile. He then went on to New York, to the State University of Syracuse, and spent four years in medical school — plus two years internship and two years residency. He then returned to Illinois, and became the house physician at Sparkle's resort…. Although Ramón Bandera knew all too well the goings-on, he kept to himself and said nothing to no one. The house doctor was on call 24 / 7, supportive to that which was held to secrecy. Whenever any of the boys got wounded, for instance, he'd patch things up and simply wouldn't report it — as required by law. To his credit, Ramón Bandera had accumulated several awards and academic honors in his file, and Sparkle trusted him with his life.

While Ramón Bandera's knowledge of the human body was extensive, human behavior was another matter. Still, the doctor of Haitian descent sat attentively before his boss, rubbing his chin thoughtfully.

"The thing's driving me crazy! I'm telling you, Ramón, it's not a bird it's a fiend, a maniacal fiend. You just don't know what it's like…those same words day in, day out: *'Don't do it; you'll be cursed for life!'* The curse is real…it grows stronger each day, and looms over me. My profits are suffering because of it…I'm at a loss."

Ramón looked sympathetic but doubtful.

"Don't you see? I've been cursed!" Sparkle spoke with passion, his hair a mess, voice strangled. "Is it possible for something to be affecting my mind?"

"Your mind…? Why, your reflexes are magnificent! You've got a superb mind! You're talking yourself into a condition that just doesn't exist."

"Then why is this happening?"

"I'm not a psychologist, and nor *do* I practice witchcraft."

"You must know something about it, being of Haitian descent!"

"That doesn't necessarily follow through."

"C'mon Ramón, I need your help! Witchcraft originated in Haiti!"

Doctor Bandera shifted uncomfortably in his seat; he let out a long sigh, and didn't care to discuss it. But did so anyway: "All I know is that a curse can make one sick. Curses have in fact been known to kill. Curses are made everyday by people, towards people, and they *are* real. Because the mind is limitless a curse will work through negative energy. Simply stated, if you believe you're cursed, you *are* cursed! You have set yourself up for a bad result."

Sparkle turned white over his bronze complexion, his mouth parched. "So what you're saying is —"

"What I'm saying is I am your doctor and your friend, and you must believe me when I tell you that nothing on earth is the matter with you. Just stop thinking about it and the curse will go away."

THE GRAND SALON WAS SITUATED OFF THE CLUBHOUSE lobby, used primarily for clandestine affairs! The clubhouse was detached from the hotel / casino, and the Grand Salon was both a piano practice room and meeting room for the boys. Apart from the scheming and conniving, Sparkle practiced diligently, playing for various events and fund raisers, the piano rhinestone bejeweled.

Sitting ridged on the bench, Sparkle struck the ivories to *Toccata and Fugue in D minor*. It was a chilling October night, a Monday, the piano in dissonant frenzy, the room all strung up with tension.

Sparkle wasn't wearing his usual sequin tux. In terms of profits, Mondays were slow, taking Mondays off. His attire was simply casual — an Armani three-piece suit. Rather, by Sparkle's standards it was casual. Still, he had on the usual bling bling: gold wristband, diamond cufflinks, ruby tiepin, pearl stickpin, emerald pendants, topaz brooches, diamond rings, diamond watch and the obligatory diamond earring from the left lobe. The stones were beautiful. More perfect stones have seldom been seen, reflecting light in a series of patterns, like a mirror ball.

A *glissando* glided up the keyboard when a slogan popped into his head: ***DONATIONS ARE BETTER THAN A LOAN TO HELP US BUY A SAXOPHONE.*** He and friend Ruby Hoffman had used the slogan as kids while panhandling. They panhandled downtown Chicago, on the southeast corner of State and Madison, where a throng hustled through and about the intersection, depositing money into their tin cup. Sparkle played the 12-bass accordion and Ruby the clarinet, and people loved it. They would generally earn up to $200 a day; a lot in those days. At day's end, Sparkle would teach Ruby how to shoplift without getting caught. Still, Ruby got caught almost every time, but not he. Not Sparkle.

Sparkle could elude the authorities even back then.

The music was building to a contrapuntal climaxed. He

worked the pedal with skill, blending close harmony deftly. The music was haunting, bringing Moose Moran to bear; the *ivories* took a pounding. He broke a sweat, his hazel eyes narrowing tightly. He sat all tense, his look crazed, like a mad "Vincent Price" at the piano.... Suddenly the alarm echoed throughout, upstaging this masterful performance.

The casino was in trouble.

He knew better than to make haste, for making haste invariably brought about mistakes and mishaps, and ultimate failure.

He inched away from the keyboard and rose from the bench, moving with leisure to his mahogany desk. Once there, he unlocked the drawer and removed a small bottle of cologne — a $21 thousand bottle. He splashed a couple drops onto his palm and rubbed it into his bronze skin. Since he had no desire to smell like the masses Sparkle flew to Paris, France, and got a personalized fragrance.

He made for the gilt mirror and produced a comb, running it through his gel laden head. For someone who wasn't particularly tall, Sparkle carried himself with a confidence that added a foot to his height. At five-feet-three, he had muscles on muscles, and had earned every one of them.

He raised his gaze to the high ceiling. "Nice artistry," he said, ignoring the inevitable robbery. Still, it was a rather nice ceiling: the glass ceiling was sculpted in Art Deco curves which yielded to a chrome circle in the center, which yielded to a stained glass dome.

He strutted out the double doors and up the stairs, to his luxury suite.

## Chapter 15
### DIRTY BIRD SPARKLE

Bad memories were like blood stains, soaking deep into the flesh and impossible to remove. The memories Sparkle had of Moose were tarnished, blood stains, seared into his soul....

Thirty years ago life was simple, people honest and straightforward. We were good-natured, always willing to lend a hand.

We smiled a lot.

The underworld wasn't so kind.

Thirty years ago John Smooth was top gun, the number one guy. John Smooth was greatly feared among his men. He was ruthlessness, and had a casual willingness to take lives and profit from the criminal endeavors his organization engaged in. John Smooth liked the finer things in life; like his penthouse office. Best view in the City of Lake Forest. Or a good steak and fine wine. That's why he bought the best talent available, from accountants to politicians to enforcers. Men whom he could trust, or whom he disposed of.... Eleven years ago Smooth was the outgoing, Sparkle the incoming.... Soon Sparkle was in over his head, needing help. He needed someone to relieve the endless days, the sleepless nights, the stress, the pain of it all. Someone to handle Operations so that he, Sparkle, could give the big picture its due....

He solicited advice from John Smooth.

Without batting an eye Smooth recommended Moose Moran...and Sparkle took his recommendation.

Moose proved A-number-one, networking neighborhoods and casing establishments...and eluding authorities. Soon the money got even greater and Moose could do no wrong, appointed vice president, privy to tight-lipped information. Entrusted with enormous sums, Moose balanced the books and stashed the stash; he hid the booty, the jewels and the cash. That is to say, he *stole* the booty, the jewels and the cash.

The theft took place six years ago, when Moose fled to Southampton, New York, and organized an outfit all his own.

Just as one thing goes wrong so goes another. Namely, "Tony Felucca," otherwise known as *Mighty Mouth!*

Tony Felucca and Sparkle had had a falling-out, bickering over the AZP heist. Seeing as how it was a five-man job Sparkle divvied up the take equally, each man getting one-fifth.

What could be fairer?

However, Mighty-Mouth (Felucca) begged to differ, insisting he should have gotten a bigger slice; i.e., since he masterminded the operation. He even stuck his neck out for the blueprints. In short, Felucca had been swindled. Kicking up a fuss, he labeled Sparkle a dirty bird, tagging him in all circles and corners.... Soon the alias Sparkle became synonymous with *Dirty Bird,* and Sparkle, at wit's end, organized a "hit" on Mighty Mouth. But never went through with it, concerned over the waves it would cause. He simply left it alone....

Too bad Felucca couldn't leave it alone.

Now, six years later, Felucca was all set on robbing Sparkle's casino, sending his minions to do the dirty work. Of course, the odds of that happening were slim to none. But Felucca didn't care about that. It was the harassment, the annoyance that mattered. Nothing more…. Least of all mob relations….

As the friendship soured so grew the hatred.

THE GUARD'S NAME WAS HARDING…BURT HARDING. AT age 23, Burt Harding had no aspirations about Security. He simply needed a job, his employment temporary…. Having seen all *Perry Masson* reruns, Harding's goal was to become an upright defense attorney, like Mason. To achieve his end, law school was a five day a week affair, his ambitions great as the day was long.

"YOU GOTTA WORK FAST — LICKETY-SPLIT! THE MOMENT that alarm goes those bars are coming down…and *no one's* getting in or out," said Henry the Itch, addressing his *compadres,* Weasel and Cannon. "The guard's gotta go up-and-over the counter and you've gotta go in after him. I mean, right after him! If you're not on his heels you'll be shut out. Game over. *Finito!* Left holding the bag…!"

"Okay, okay — we know all that! You've covered *it* a hundred times. What happens next?" asked Weasel, twitching his neck and shifting his eyes like a ferret, a skunk, a fur-bearing creature.

Henry tightened his eyes from behind the sunglasses; he locked his gaze on Weasel, the little man with the long neck. Cannon cringed at Henry blowing his cool, botching three months of intense planning. But rather than blow his cool Henry simply *flung* his hand to his shoulder, and scratched. Weasel flinched, his eyes pinned wide. Henry said: "You keep an eye on the cashiers while Cannon and I haul the guard into the back room. Think you can you handle it?"

Weasel offered *no* response, standing his ground; he glared at Henry, the man towering over him, and tried to control his twitchy eyelid.

The senior cashier nonchalantly studied the hulking lummox and his snarling cronies. The three of them were in the vicinity, and the instant cashier Agnes heard that gravelly voice she knew trouble was lurking. Despite the disguise, nothing could hide Henry's deep and wheezy voice — like a trombone with laryngitis. Nor could anything hide his square-shoulders...his deep chest. Neither could the sunglasses nor fuzzy goatee. With a six-four frame, Henry the Itch was in a class all his own, and Agnes knew precisely with whom she was dealing: Tony Felucca's boys....

Like most casinos, the Roman Empire was loud and noisy and Agnes didn't catch everything, just various phrases: *bars down, guard, over the counter, back room.* To compensate for the din, Henry elevated his voice, and Agnes — zeroing in like sonar — had no problem fingering them.

Fast approaching 11:00 PM Agnes Erickson went about her duties, keeping one eye on the money and the other on the thugs. She monitored their whereabouts, them lingering at the ATM machines: Weasel studied the machines, Cannon whistled unconcernedly, and Henry scratched and clawed, as if he'd forgotten his itch medicine. All the while Guard Harding was surrounded.

All the while Guard Harding was clueless....

AGNES ONCE WORKED AT LAKE FOREST, AT SPARKLE'S underground casino. It was there, Lake Forest, Agnes had gotten familiar with Henry, Weasel and Cannon — three small time crooks. She therefore knew something was up, throwing the switch beneath the counter — the panic-switch on the left. She could have thrown the right switch but *that* switch was for hotel security, and Agnes didn't feel good about that. Knowing this was a job for Sparkle, Agnes rang in her boss, the Grand Salon, the room in which Sparkle had spent most of his time. If for any reason he wasn't in the Grand Salon a signal would cut into his cell phone and, either way, he'd get the message.

## Chapter 16
## THE CASINO ROBBERY

AGNES ERICKSON WENT ABOUT HER DUTIES, WHEN AT 11:00 PM time hit the ground running. Weasel leapt over the counter, Henry and Cannon going in next, Guard Harding glued to their sides, the bars rolling down just after them.... People were falling over themselves, running to the exits in confusion, darkness falling out of a clear blue sky. Still, gaming forged on, hard-core gamblers making wagers as if nothing were awry....

Had it not been for Albert Brook — Weasel's nephew — the caper would not have stood a chance. Thanks to Albert Brook, the casino alarm went off without a hitch, rattling bones and knocking teeth loose. When Weasel presented his nephew the anti-jamming problem, Albert suggested a wireless computer, modem, and password generator. Albert, who majored in computer software, assured nothing would go wrong which, in essence, made Albert Brook the *real* brains of it all....

While Henry acted like the *big cheese,* Weasel thought he only smelled like it.

\* \* \*

AT THE MERCY OF HENRY AND CANNON, GUARD HARDING was hauled into the vault, forced at gunpoint to sack money — his third week on the job and already in more trouble than his entire student tenure.

Weasel, meantime, held the cashiers at bay, his nickel-plated .45 waving persuasively. Still, Agnes Erickson wasn't about to keep quiet, turning to the little man with the shifty eyes. "There's no way you're getting away with this. You'll get ten to fifteen!"

Weasel gave Agnes the sandpaper side of his tongue. "I don't think so. We *are* getting away with it, and *Dirty Bird's* gonna eat crow. Now shut-it or I'll turn you into Swiss cheese!"

WHEN ONE IS WITH NATURE ONE IS "AT ONE" WITH Nature....

The majestic elm stood outside the cash room, the tree cresting fully, branches bending in the wind. Sparkle, dressed in black, sat high atop the tree, the sky hazy and moonless. By way of auto-relaxation, he closed his eyes and regulated his breathing, and lowered his blood pressure...thereby stimulating his Psychic Reception Area.

His mind's eye went right to work, dialing in on Henry, Weasel and Cannon.

THE AREA OUT BACK WAS TEEMING WITH SHADOWS, NOT A soul in sight. The door suddenly shot open, when light pitched across the thoroughfare, erasing shadows. Weasel pressed the gun's muzzle into the small of Harding's back, forcing him to lead the way. In an awkward attempt to flee, the guard hastened his stride. Weasel warned: "Not so fast, bub, slow it down or you'll be sucking wind through your esophagus...!" Harding slowed his pace and Cannon, closing the door behind him, brought back the shadows. They removed their sunglasses and felt spied upon, sharpening their vigilance — their heads turned side to side, like watching a tennis match.... They walked in tandem, Cannon grasping a gun in one hand, the loot his other. They headed down a T-junction, the shape of the "T" obscured by dim lighting and a moonless sky.

Three crooks were getting away with piles of money and Security was nowhere in the area. Just how this could be...?

Henry and Cannon crept low to the ground, Weasel at full height, forcing the guard to show the way.

They happened by the sprawling tree, dead leaves churning.

*Something flashed!*

It happened suddenly and right before them. They pitched back, arms twirling like pinwheels. A *thing* of sorts appeared from out of the blue, their jaws dropping, eyes popping. Some *thing* landed cleanly before them, hitting the ground with a nimble grace...a lithe. Some thing in black...some thing not of this world!

Their eyes went soggy and wet, the thing all smeary and blurry. Still, no mistaking the aquiline nose, the jet-black hair...the short physique and hazel eyes — *deadly* eyes!

A terse question ripped across their minds: *"What is it"?*

A gusty wind kicked up the thing's scent.... Having decided on likeable colors, food tastes, interests and the like, the thing's aroma therapist had determined that Chinese yam, adventitious root, and foxglove had best suited the thing's high-strung, savvy, and quick to take offense personality; hence, all going into the mix.

At $7 thousand an ounce the fragrance was a true expression of its soul:

*Sparkle!*

Sparkle folded his arms across his sculpted chest, his eyes boring a hole through Henry the Itch. He spoke with confidence. "Don't know when to quit, do you? How could you expect to get away with this? You're just a bunch of idiots!"

Henry eyed him with contempt. "They say you're pretty solid. Still starching your legs to keep them from wobbling? Incidentally, how's the weather down there...? I eat pipsqueaks for breakfast. Now stand aside or we'll twist you into a pretzel!"

"Nothin' doing...! Hand over the money and I might go easy on you."

"What…tickle us with Pigeon feathers?" Henry's pasty-skinned cronies started to snicker.

"I'll break every bone in your bodies and *then* I'll get angry!"

Henry whisked a hand up to his shoulder, and merely scratched. Sparkle failed to flinch, missing his cue. Henry balked, his forehead creasing into a scowl, his brows coming together darkly. He squared his shoulders and elevated his voice, like one addressing an audience in an ancient coliseum. "Seems Dirty Bird wants to rock-and-roll, boys…! What say we oblige him?"

"Stop!" yelled Sparkle. "You might wanna think it over. Not fair…*only* three of you! "

Fired up, Weasel released Harding and the three of them came in fast, converging as one: they ran in like *matadors,* slamming into each other like *picadors,* all morphing into *cuspidors.* They reeled hard to the ground, Sparkle all but disappearing into the air, like wings on heels; he descended on Henry and Cannon, grabbing both their heads and ramming them together, the two of them going out like lights, moaning softly on the cold ground.

Weasel shot up with a vengeance, raring to go; he took aim when Sparkle kicked the gun out of his grasp, the pistol landing just two feet in front of Harding. Weasel flew down to the gun when Harding kicked it under a pile of dead leaves.

Weasel rose in a mad flurry of arms, and lunged into the guard. But Sparkle had other plans, yanking Weasel up by the back of his collar and seat of his pants and sweeping him off his feet. Sparkle spun Weasel around in a circle, Weasel's torso arched with the ground, his body close to Sparkle's — near the center of rotation. Suddenly Sparkle extended his right foot and, bending his knees, hurled Weasel through the air like a slingshot, Weasel catapulting 10 feet before hitting the grass heels over head, somersaulting across the grounds before skidding to a stop. He lay twisted and contorted, his body scraped and bruised.

Weak and dizzy from the head butt just earlier, Cannon climbed sluggishly to his feet; he elevated his .380 SIG and Sparkle hit the ground, the gun's hammer falling suddenly, the round dinging the tree just above and behind Sparkle's head.

Harding chopped the gun out of Cannon's grasp; Cannon tightened with anger, backhanding the guard's face with a *thwack!* Harding winced, and Sparkle — up and about — ran in at a full sprint; he vaulted high into the air, his leg fully extended. Sparkle sailed into Cannon, slamming his outstretched jogger into the thug's head squarely and ferociously —

*Wham, bam!*

The two-bit crook teetered and tottered, his eyes rolling to the back of his head; he fell hard to the ground, flat and sprawled.

Henry rose to full height and, clutching the money bag like a battering ram, got back into the game. He ran in at top speed, bolstering his confidence with banshee-like screams, aiming for Sparkle's solar plexus…intent on making a direct hit.

Sparkle stooped low, feign-cocking his arms. The six-foot-four man ran in fast, thrusting his sturdy bag when — overbalanced as he was — tumbled over Sparkle's hunched stance, striking the ground in an explosive thud. Facedown, the aroma of grass filled Henry's nostrils, his right arm bent out at an awkward angle, languishing in pain.

Low pitched moans filled the air, the thugs helpless on the cold, damp ground.

The head of security, Bob Stevens, wasn't at all troubled by any of this. He did as he was told, monitoring the situation before ringing in the police. He wasn't expected to do more. All Sparkle wanted was time enough to break heads. Ensuring the bad guys got their just desserts was self-indulging.

Sparkle whipped out a pocket mirror and comb and paused to fix his hair. He studied his image, grooming his fully enriched head with a practiced sweep of the comb.

A fleet of cruisers pulled onto the roadside…. Doors flung open, when a squadron of police tackled three moaning bandits in one fell swoop. Coworkers gathered around Harding, doling out high-fives and hearty pats on the back.

Three media vans pulled up when Sparkle slipped out of the event and into shadow. Late for the eleven o'clock meeting, he headed back to the clubhouse.

## Chapter 17
## MEET THE BOYS

Ace Flint bore a scared cheek. The scar was jagged and hideous and resulted from a boyhood accident; it rendered a stern, cold look. People thought smiling made his face ache. Still, started everyday out with a smile — just to get it over with.

Ace was an expert marksman…a dead-shot, best trigger-man in the business of crime. He wore a cutting-edge suit, which hung handsomely on his well-built frame. His tie was Armani; shoes Italian leather, polished to brilliance. He didn't drink and nor did he smoke. He finished high school with a scarred face and rarely smiled. Still, had no problem keeping a woman! With two wives and a hundred girlfriends, Ace was a true ace.

Gregory "Ace" Flint was a confidence man, his demeanor hardened by the underworld.

Those who knew him wouldn't dare cross him.

Those who didn't know him were the lucky ones.

* * *

RON LEVY WAS THIEF BY STEALTH — YOUR COMMON everyday pickpocket! With long fingers and a light touch, Ron Levy could swipe the wings off a bee without a shred of evidence. In fact, it was picking pockets that led to Ace Flint. It began at a mall in Park Ridge, Illinois, the day sunny and bright. Ace was in men's wear, when a voice in his head warned against wallets in pockets. He no more than reached for his wallet when he and Ron shook hands. With "stealing" as a common thread, they teamed up, both into something more profitable than picking one's pocket.

They were a two-man crime wave, doing Sparkle's dirty work and leaving no trail.

The FBI had labeled it a white collar crime…

Mortgage Fraud!

Mortgage Fraud was a lucrative scam that made Ace and Ron — rather, Sparkle — a lot of money.

A quitclaim deed was a common document found at any office supply store. A quitclaim deed was used to transfer property. In the wrong hands, the document was nothing short of a license to steal. The con would simply put the property under the real owner's name, falsify the signature, and then record the deed at the County Court House. Next, using false identification, receive a substantial bank loan.

EDDY BLACK COULD WELL HAVE BEEN BURIED THREE years! He looked years beyond his time, the corners of his eyes furrowed and wrinkled — enough wrinkles to hold a three-day rain. At 34, Eddy Black was a narcotics junkie, his face shallow and gaunt. His eyes were sunken, steeped in crow's feet on crow's feet. He had dull yellow skin — like the color of old newspapers. His hair was gray and receding, cheeks rawboned and hollow. He did however have muscles — tucked inside his bones. Thanks to gum disease, all his teeth had been pulled. However, the hearing aid worked like a charm. At six-one, Black weighed one fifty-eight drunk, one twenty-six sober.

Eddy Black needed a moniker, something to identify with…. To fill the bill, Black was dubbed "Crack."

Crack's briefcase was filled with drugs, drugs of all kinds. He knew their properties and side effects, and also the drug lords and pimps — the rank and file of street gangs. To expedite his efforts, Crack had two understudies: Bruce Barkley and Al Jerome. Bruce and Al were college dropouts, their job simply to chew the fat with bouncers and learn which gangs supplied the city. They also maintained records — the catalyst for pushing narcotics through the toughest neighborhoods of Chicago without as much as a scratch.... Securing drugs was easy, staying off drugs *wasn't*. Thanks to Crack, Bruce and Al had no problem discerning the ill effects of drugs, deeming drugs off limits. They wouldn't even take cough syrup.

Not *one* aspirin!

THE GRAND SALON WAS LADEN WITH CROWN MOLDING AND red and gold velvet, the piano jewel encrusted....

Ron paced back and forth, like a tiger in a cage, his heels clicking on the Italian marble. A fat cigar hung from the side of his mouth, gray smoke consuming his path.... He stopped pacing and lowered his gaze to Ace, sitting on the couch. Ron opened his mouth as if to say something, but said nothing, and resumed his back and forth stride. The midnight hour was approaching, and the Grand Salon was missing some people.

Ace watched as housekeeping set assorted cold cuts on the coffee table. The edibles were arranged neatly on an English silver tray, vintage china aligning all around it. The help retreated, closing the doors behind them. Ace rose, and poured hot coffee into a cup; he returned to his seat.

Ron ground to a stop, his face beat red. He whirled into his partner. "What on earth's keeping him?"

"Give the guy a break, will ya? For once he's late — big deal! Sparkle's never late."

"Crack...! I mean Crack, not Sparkle! It's almost twelve...where is he?"

"So what's new? Crack's always late!"

"Sparkle oughta kick his drugged-out ass!"

Ace rubbed the white scar on his cheek, and sipped black coffee. Ron raised his gaze to the geometrically carved ceiling — he studied the Art Deco curves and chrome circles yielding to a glass dome. He lowered his gaze and drew on his cigar — coughed, and resumed scuffing the floor.

The great doors clanged open and Ron skidded to a stop, dropping ashes. Ace turned sharply in his seat, almost spilling coffee.

Crack stormed inside with one briefcase and two bloodshot eyes; he blundered to his boss's desk. Bruce Barkley and Al Jerome trailed behind, hoping Crack would somehow get out of the beating due him: Sparkle's sure-fire remedy for tardiness.

Standing afore the desk, Crack fronted the back of the high-back chair, turned halfway around.... "I know I'm late, Boss, but it's not my fault! We were chased by this green car, three black dudes after my drug dough, see, but I gave 'em the slip — saved all of it!" Crack held up his briefcase, all but expecting the chair to deem him a hero.

Bruce moseyed to the front of the chair and copped a peek. "Not here," said Bruce, chomping on a wad of gum.

"Honest Boss, that's just how it happened," said Crack, ignoring Bruce.

"Hel-lo!" Bruce's voice rose, and waved a hand at his supervisor. "I said he's not here!" Bruce swiveled the chair around, giving Crack a bird's-eye view. Crack's face contorted, his yellow skin flashing pink. He glanced over his shoulder, and saw Ron blowing smoke rings, studying his lame excuse.

"Where'd he go?" asked Crack.

"They abducted him."

"Who...?"

"Sparkle, who do you think? Little green men in flying saucers hauled him away!" Ron's astonishment was dripping with sarcasm.

Crack didn't appreciate the mockery. "That's funny — real funny! Look, I'm just telling you what happened, how these green men in a black...I, I mean black men in a green —"

Sparkle stormed into the room, his eyes burning, seething with anger. He strode across the floor, checking his stride at the hophead. "You were late!"

"Yes, but —" was all Crack had said when a hand flashed, slapping him on either side of the face. Crack rubbed his cheeks, his eyes befuddled. "Those hands are deadly, Boss; they can really hurt somebody!"

"Oh, really…? Y'think?" Sparkle balled up his fingers, a cloud of tensions simmering. He suddenly drove his fist into Crack's solar plexus, doubling him over. A second later shot up with clasped hands, ramming a double fist into Crack's lower jaw and lifting him off the floor, his gangly body slamming against the deck with a brutal thud! He lay flat and sprawled, and emitted a dull, aching moan. Al froze like a mannequin, and Bruce swallowed his gum.

Jolts of electricity ran up and down spines, people flabbergasted.

Al flexed his foot, poised to aid his supervisor. But then suddenly he and Sparkle locked gazes, when Al looked down at his chest, as though his dark blue tie had suddenly become interesting.

Sparkle picked up a stainless steel pitcher and walked it over to Crack, dousing him with water. He turned to Al. "Help him up!" Sparkle set down the pitcher and Al helped Crack get back on his feet.

Sparkle made for the bar, whereby pouring whisky into a shot glass; he pulled on the drink. He set down the glass, backhanded his lips, and strutted up to the gold-framed mirror; he studied his reflection before running a comb through his head.

Meantime, Bruce and Al arranged five upholstered armchairs in front of the desk. Crack removed his waterlogged coat, exposing his shoulder harness and gun. He then fell into a chair next to Al, and everyone but Ace — who remained on the couch — followed suit, leaving the end chair open…. Sparkle trained his eyes on Crack, who was rubbing the large red welt growing on his chin. "Any questions regarding time…?"

"No, Boss…eleven o'clock."

"Don't forget, if you know what's good for you. The next time I'll hit you so hard on the head you'll be able to ride half fare!"

Crack blinked back tears. "There won't be a next time." He turned to his trainees and assessed blame. "You heard the man...now quit causing me to be late!" Bruce and Al sat in stunned bewilderment, utterly confounded.

Sparkle relaxed his tension. "So tell me, Crack...what *have* you to bestow?"

Crack rose, and staggered up to the plate, briefcase in tow. Still, unlike before, when Crack was new and on edge, he learned how to settle down...if only because the "take" got him in good with the boss.... Crack extended his briefcase; Sparkle took it, and snapped it open.

Crack stood all smug.

Sparkle froze, his breathing labored. He pounded his desk with a clenched fist. Everyone pitched back, and Sparkle turned red in the face. He raised his glower to Crack. "This some kinda joke?" He grabbed a handful of paraphernalia and showed Crack what he'd given him. Icy trickles slithered into Crack's underwear and Al shot out of his seat, bolting out the door. He ran through the clubhouse lobby, darting around guests and out the building...to the car — for the other briefcase.

A "diamond" graphic was printed on each and every wrapper, a trademark, which *indirectly* linked Sparkle to the illicit product. When it came to narcotics Crack knew all their properties and side effects, and, how to get them out on the street.

He just didn't know one briefcase from the other.

Crack stepped aside and Ace, taking his place, forked over his briefcase. Sparkle clicked it open and removed a sheet of paper. Ace studied his boss's expression, his bubbly expression. Sparkle said: "Nice, real nice!"

The paper chronicled "false" real estate purchases. It listed locations, square footage, market value, and rightful owner(s). It also listed banks and loans issued.

"It's all cleaned and pressed," said Ace, referencing the money inside.

Ace knew somebody who owned a Dry Cleaning franchise. For a nominal fee this someone would even clean money. A lot of legitimate businesses were in fact money-laundering fronts for organized crime. Namely, Mafia and Chinese, peppered with an American home grown variety.

Sparkle was most pleased.

Ace proceeded back to the sofa, and suddenly the doors banged open. Heads turned into Al, moving hastily across the floor with a briefcase plastered against his heaving chest. He extended the case to Crack when Sparkle said, "I'll take that!" Al sidestepped Crack and surrendered it to Sparkle.

Al returned to his seat, and Crack braced for the worst, for nothing seemed to go right.

Sparkle no sooner opened the case than his eyes glowed green, straps of money dancing in his head.

## Chapter 18
## BLACK THE CRACK

THE OPIUM POPPY WAS THE SOURCE OF HEROIN, registering 94 percent pure at street level....

"Mule" was a term used to describe narcotics smuggler. Joel Rucker was Sparkle's mule...and a dozen other crime bosses. State officials were puzzled, Sparkle one step ahead, always managing to slip by. An essential part of Sparkle's "sneakiness" was Joel Rucker. Joel Rucker was a licensed pilot who lived on a ranch in Imperial Beach, just south of San Diego. The drugs came from Columbia, where Rucker flew a single engine Cessna low enough at the boarder so as to *not* show up on radar.

The contraband arrived in the wee hours, whereby loaded in a white Ford Bronco. With "Park Maintenance" decaled on the sides of it, Rucker — attired in baggy coveralls and heavy-soled boots — drove to a remote region at Balboa Park and placed the cargo inside a hallowed-out tree; the cargo was later replaced with a package containing $50 thousand by Rucker's contact. The drugs were distributed to Crack and others and, to throw off the Feds,

Sparkle bypassed Rucker and dealt strictly with the contact.

Like most pushers, Crack was a first time offender. Because of America's war on drugs, 80 percent of first time offenders served time. Following an all night binge, Crack was pulled over for erratic driving. He was charged with DUI and narcotics possession, and did time in the Illinois prison system on drug-related convictions — all of which revealed a chronic need for drugs and the failure of good advice and hopeful therapy.

Crack's family couldn't understand why he turned to drugs. Ever since high school he'd been a light social user, nothing more. Maybe it was pressure from school or maybe to escape his mother's yapping. Certainly not a habit! He couldn't remember when it had turned to the hard stuff.... Now the drugs were important. Now, he might never stop.

There was once a time when Bruce and Al were articulate and bright, fiercely honest, loyal, conscientious to a fault. They were college sophomores who'd simply gone off the beaten path, dropping out of school and working for Crack, earning some fast coin and making some fast getaways.

ANN FORTE SAT BEFORE A MAGNIFICATION MIRROR; SHE powdered and brushed and powdered and brushed some more. She stopped powdering/brushing, and gave pause to her pearls, wondering how South Sea pearls would go with her lightly tanned complexion. "Yes, I think so," she muttered.

Her dress was elegant, fit for a queen, showcasing a synthetic fur hem and quilted lapels and hand embroidery. Her bracelet was gem studded, diamond earrings adorning her slender face and ear-length bob...almost every finger ringed.

Ann inherited her aunt's macaw — a vivid parrot with a regal beak and talons strong enough to rip flesh much less snarl hair. She therefore had her hair cropped short, preventing the *clawed* shoulder-hugger from tangling anything.

She lifted the pearl necklace from a bed of black velvet and clasped it round her white throat.

\* \* \*

SPARKLE SIPPED BLACK COFFEE AND SCANNED HIS MEN, his eyes tight and squinty…. He spoke with careful deliberation. "On October the ninth, this Saturday, Moose is going down on Larkin's. And he doesn't know I'm onto him."

Bruce and Al swung into each other, their eyes twisted. Al turned to Sparkle. "Excuse me, Boss, but what is Larkin's?"

"Larkin's is a jewelry house in New York City. It's where Moose plans to haul away the Charles O'Leary collection, the Hutchins' gem, and plus a boatload of stones valued at over twenty mil." Sparkle cocked an eye. "Nice down payment on what he owes me, wouldn't you say?"

Bruce and Al sat in gaping silence, their open-mouth patterns identical. Once the shock wore off, Bruce said. "You mean he *robbed* you?"

Sparkle bristled. "'Rob'? Wrong term! 'Steal' is more like it. Moose is too smart to rob me."

"But what if he doesn't cooperate?" asked Bruce.

"Doesn't cooperate?" Everyone started to laugh, except Sparkle, who found nothing amusing…. Once the hilarity let up, Sparkle continued: "Let's just say if I don't get the Hutchins' gem, Moose is in a real gem of a jam!" Sparkle's face went dark. He clenched a fist and pounded his desk, the thud emphasizing anger. "Back at Lake Forest, Moose sat in my chair. My right-hand guy! I trusted him, and for what…?" He took a deep breath and relaxed his tension. "But we all make mistakes. And Moose was a mistake, a big mistake."

"How do you know all this?" asked Al. "I mean, about Larkin's?"

"Through David Siegel, my contact. I've got Siegel working for him…his *valet.*"

"That's pretty cleaver," said Bruce, nodding in reverence. "So when do we lea —"

A loud click emanated, when heads swerved into the door. Ann stood framed in the doorway, her hand gloved in leather. She was picture-perfect, like a high fashion model. A hush fell over the room, and a second later she sauntered across the floor, her curvaceous body sashaying in rhythm. At five-feet-six inches tall, Ann's lean build drew more than a few second glances. She wore a form fitted gown, which accentuated her hips. Dangerous hips! Sparkle's temperature rose...or maybe it was the room. Ann had that effect on Sparkle — and rooms. Her hair was golden, face radiant, overshadowing the 36-inch parrot swaying on her shoulder. While Sparkle had little time for his wife, he did however enjoy his wife's company; especially when it was important for his wife to be seen hanging from his arm. This just wasn't the time. Nor was it the time to start an argument. So he let it slide and rolled with the punches.

Ann tossed her purse down on the end chair. She raised her gloved hand to Cash, the parrot hopping aboard. Ann eased down to the chair, her rump pressing into her purse. She moved the purse aside and settled into her seat, her bird-hand resting on the chair arm. Cash sat motionless and silent, and Sparkle, gazing into his wife's blue-grays, melted in her beauty, her cheekbones vibrant; her lips were ruby red, her face an oval of creamy-white skin demanding to be caressed. Cash too was enthralled — but with the man at the desk. Sparkle saw the parrot's glare and tried not to let on. He couldn't let on. He was, after all, a man with whom hundreds of people called "boss." His mind was sharp, brilliant, his ego huge. He was ambitious and shrewd, ruthless to the core, and right now the most dangerous man in the world. Still, Cash wasn't intimidated, presenting its notorious stare. Its evil eye...! The bird suddenly flashed up with a witchlike cry. And this cry was echoed by another. Sparkle flinched, crackling and crumbling under the watchful eye of the parrot. He sweated coldly. He shut his eyes and tried to relax. A moment later, opened his eyes and put the bird behind him. He got a grip and forged on. But the parrot had thrown him for a loop, and he'd forgotten the last minutes — too bad records *weren't* kept (for obvious reasons). Just then Bruce chimed in with the question he'd tried asking earlier. "When are we leaving?"

"I want everyone here tomorrow afternoon, three p.m. sharp. We'll take two cars, and depart at —"

"Don't do it; you'll be 'cursed' for life!" said Cash, its voice deep and guttural, reverberating throughout the room. Realizing he'd been cursed, Sparkle froze, his heart lodged in his throat. He calmly folded his hands, and took his doctor's advice, ignoring the parrot's curse. "As I was saying…we'll leave here at four."

Unbeknownst to Sparkle, Crack had completely dozed, his eyes closed shut.

"Excuse me, sir," said Al, "may I ask a question?"

*"Shoot"* was all Sparkle had said.

Crack leapt out of his chair and, yanking out his Colt .45, began to yell in a stupor: "I'll punch holes big enough for birds to fly through!" He flailed his gun-hand and everyone ran for cover. Ann, however, kept her cool and didn't budge; to herself, dared Crack to try and start something…! Excitement ran rampant, Sparkle dropping beneath his desk, Cash ruffling feathers and squawking hysterically. Just at the height of madness the room fell silent. Crack, realizing he'd goofed, holstered his gun and wilted like a flower.

The bird let out a throaty squawk, breaking the silence.

The utility door slowly opened, when Bruce stepped back into the room. Ace crawled out from underneath the coffee table, and Al and Ron eased out from behind the piano. Everyone returned to their chairs when Sparkle, rising from beneath his desk, lumbered up to Crack, eyes cold and dark. Crack lowered his gaze to his boss's glare when, just then, the parrot reiterated its sentiments: "Don't do it; you'll be cursed for life!"

Sparkle swung his head into Cash, and let out an explosive snort. He turned back to Crack, and suddenly a hand flashed, slapping Crack not once but twice across the face. "And there's plenty more where that came from!" Sparkle's brows came together darkly, his face frigid. "The next time you pull a stunt like this I'll twist your head so completely around, that when you're walking north you'll be looking south!" Crack rubbed his red cheeks, his eyes soggy wet. Sparkle returned to his desk and

119

Crack eased down to his chair.

Sparkle locked his gaze on Ann; under normal circumstances he would have swooned. Under these circumstances, beauty was an afterthought. He said, "Was nice of Jane to leave you her parrot..." He narrowed his eyes, his blood boiling.

"Wasn't it, though?" Ann felt slighted, climbing out of her chair and placing Cash on her shoulder; she saw her way to the door and departed.

Sparkle picked up four pencils and, two in each hand, thumbed them in halves. A wild look washed over him, mouths falling in astonishment.... He spoke in strangled tones: "Sorry Boys, but that bird is killing me! It's not even a bird; it's a monster, a beast with wings. A lowdown, contemptible beast! A detestable, accursed beast, nothing more! A four-flushin', mean spirited — *bea-uuutiful* work, Ron...!" The double-doors opened suddenly, when Sparkle quickly turned to Ron. "Your work is simply *beautiful!*" Ann re-entered, and made for her purse, which was left behind. She picked up her purse while steadying Cash on her shoulder. She turned to her husband. "Sorry for the intrusion, dear...."

"That's quite alright, Ann, we all make mistakes. Nobody's perfect." His tone was menacing, spoken through clenched teeth; he resembled the Frankenstein monster trying to resemble "Mr. Rogers."

The parrot was offended: "Don't do it; you'll be cursed for life!" Ann strolled to the exit, the parrot all frenzied: "Don't do it; you'll be cursed for life...!" Ann departed, closing the doors behind her.

Sparkle went berserk, scrambling his hair and slamming books, scattering his desk. His men were taken aback, their mouths wide-open, their stares glassy.

His hair entangled, Sparkle cleared his throat and slowed down his breathing, his chest rising and falling evenly. "Sorry for the outburst, boys, but — well.... He sighed mightily. "I've been hexed...! With your help, I'll stop it from becoming the final chapter of my career...! I just can't go it alone. But not now!

Now you should be thinking of New York. We'll discuss this bird thing some other time.... If there are no further questions, that concludes —"

"I have a question," said Al.

"What is it?" Sparkle chose his words carefully.

"Why mess around with Moose when we can pull our own caper?"

"The boys and I used to pull plenty of jobs, and the pay off *was* great. But the planning is endless, and I just don't have the time. Furthermore, Moose owes me and, frankly, that's reason enough. Now if there are no other questions you're free to go...."

## Chapter 19
## THAT'S HIM!

MICHAEL BAGLEY TOOK AN EARLY INTEREST IN PHYSICS. It began in grade school and piqued in high school, pressing on to the Massachusetts Institute of Technology (MIT).... Having obtained a PhD in engineering, he landed a job at Johnson, as a space technician. His work in demo software was noteworthy, showcasing mechanical design, systems integration, radiation shielding, and prototype development. He also helped in the advancement of space robotics and mirror technology. Not many could boast such a prowess. Still — despite all that — Michael Bagley had a rather serious problem. His problem was maturity, as Michael Bagley couldn't seem to act his age.

Michael, a member of Robert's former team, was just too much like Victor Evans — Mary's alcoholic stepfather. Like Victor, Michael was pushy and controlling, his mouth big and empty, Mary all peeved and aggravated. She preferred the Robert Smith type — the "gentle as a mountain fog" type.... Michael just didn't get it, making Robert the brunt of jokes, attacking him at every turn. Especially at the end of Robert's tenure, exploiting his delirium condition. He even painted Robert as a skinflint, a miser of the worse kind.

Mary Evans had a shapely figure, which punctuated her regal walk; it earned her the title Queen of the Water Cooler. Her puppy-like eyes highlighted a set of full lips and dainty nose. She had short hair, which framed her sleek face; she could excite the sun on a cloudy day. Hardly a wonder everyone on the team had asked her out. Everyone, that is, but Robert Smith, who didn't think he'd get to first base.

Upon Robert's discharged, computer specialist Mary was up against it. Michael was out of control and Mary, on the receiving end, fell behind in circuit board designs. In fact, Michael too fell behind; i.e., the *designs* he had on Mary's circuits...! She put in for a transfer but was denied, leaving no choice but to retire early. Upon discharge, she moved to Long Island, New York, settling into a gated community — a fair distance from Rockford...and Robert.


ONE FLAMING CANDLE PER BOOTH WAS SCAECELY ENOUGH to alight the room.

Fitzwilly's Gourmet was a Manhattan landmark, where tourist frequented and locals prospered. The dining area was posh, replete with crystal and white linen and silver tableware. The maitre d' escorted guests to their tables, where cutlery pinged against china and low conversation hung in the air.

Mary Evans enjoyed a night out with friends Rick and Joyce Sanders, both in their thirties. Rick, a smartly dressed man in a tailored suit, was accompanied by wife Joyce, adorned in silk and black satin. Sipping coffee, they chitchatted on a variety of topics when the conversation turned to NASA.

"...No problem, because if the main goes down a backup will automatically kick in," said Mary. "Any more than two computers are problematic. It's incumbent upon all engineers to reduce payload. That's really what it's all about."

"Oh...I see. Makes sense, I suppose," said Joyce, shrugging

her shoulders. "So why *did* you retire?"

"I didn't want to retire, but there was this problem —"

"Really?" said Rick, cutting Mary off mid-sentence. "What was 'his' name?"

"Michael Bagley.... Mike was just too aggressive, just too pushy and — well — getting out was really my only option."

Joyce and Rick turned into each another, and wondered what the other was thinking.

Rick slid a look in Mary's direction. "You mean harassment?"

"What else?" Mary heaved a sigh.

"You miss him, don't you?" asked Joyce.

"What, Michael?"

"Not Michael...your team leader, Robert Smith. That's what it really comes down to, isn't it?"

"Well, yeah, I suppose. I mean, what girl wouldn't? Problem was he never noticed me."

"But Mary, the way you describe him...this Robert fella sounds like a nutcase," said Rick.

"No, Robert's not a nut. I mean sure, got a few marbles rolling around, but he's not a nut."

"For my money, he's a nut!"

Her voice rose slightly. "He's not a nut...!" She suddenly turned all dreamy, her eyes glazed and dazed. "All I ever wanted was to cast my line in the sea of matrimony and catch me a Roberto. But he never even knew I existed." She drew a sigh. "I'm afraid that in that great furnace of romance, my pilot light has gone out."

"No it hasn't," said Joyce, "just turn up the burner!"

"Turn up the burner? 'Fraid not... Not that easy."

"Rick and Joyce lifted their cups in unison and sipped; they stole glances at each other.

Rick set his cup down and regarded Mary with earnest. "You know, Mary, you have to really know that special someone if you want them to take notice."

"What do you mean?"

"I mean you don't know this guy."

"Sure I do!"

"Well then, let's put it to a test…"

"Test…? What kinda test?"

"A simple litmus test…just a few questions to see how well you know him."

"Okay, fine…guess it won't hurt."

"Rick fell silent, pondering just how to go about this…. Finally he said: "So tell me, Mary, is Robert the aggressive type?"

"No, that's not him."

"Is he the shy type?"

She rolled her eyes and rubbed her chin. *"Nooo…not him…"*

"Does he live in the fast lane? You know…the live-for-today type?"

"Not *him.*"

"I see…then how 'bout the snooty type?"

"Not *him.*"

"The sneaky type…?"

"Not *him.*"

"The *Casanova* type…?"

"Not *him.*"

"Well now, there you have it…"

"Have what? What *does* it all mean?"

"Means he's a nut…"

"THAT'S *HIM!*"

IT WAS NIGHTTIME, OCTOBER THE 7th, WHEN SOMETHING unexpected happened. Mary will never forget October 7th — the night mascara ran down her face, smudging those knockout cheekbones. She'd been standing out in the cold, gazing up at the stars, thinking about Robert; she'll never look at the night sky the same way…. It all started with e-mail — NASA's e-mail invitation to the annual convention. The convention was slated for New York City, not far from where she resided…. If only Robert would show….

\* \* \*

AN UNSETTLING THOUGHT FLITTED THROUGH SPARKLE'S head: *Any woman who spends time with a bird can't be trusted responsibly.*

Before leaving for New York, Sparkle placed butler Rupert in charge of operations.

**Chapter 20**
**THE ETERNAL CODE**

O CTOBER THE 8th FOUND SPARKLE JUST OUTSIDE
Cleveland, on his way to New York City.

Early that morning Rupert Bennett drew Ann's bath, adding
essential oils and rose petals for health and comfort.... Upon
bathing in the privacy of her suite, Ann checked Charity Teas,
which weren't up for another week. With little on her plate, a
leisurely swim seemed just the thing, soliciting The Help to move
Cash down poolside — despite the "closed" pool. Thanks to chief
butler Rupert, the fairytale princess managed around the 10 AM
opening.

RUPERT BENNETT UNLOCKED THE CLUBHOUSE POOL,
allowing housekeeping inside; they set the cage down between two
plastic chairs and retreated, the self-closing door echoing shut
behind them. The heated pool was equipped with timed, fiber
optic lighting, the water changing colors randomly. The parrot
peered past the bars, locking a silvery eye on the hued water, its

head bobbing and weaving. Ann removed her sheer robe and made for the water, her bikini barely legal. She entered the pool slowly, her limbs trailing languidly, legs buoying in the cushion of water...a cavity of warm splendor. The foxy beauty looked at her diamond watch, which read a quarter of eight — roughly two hours before the pool opening. "Cash!" she called out, her voice echoic. Cash ruffled feathers and purred like a kitten; it pranced back and forth on the perch.

She looked up, and saw caretaker Hoskins hosing down the ceramic tiles. She wondered if he'd dare hose down Cash. A voice buzzed in her head: *Not if he knows what's good for him!* She gave Hoskins no mind and, leaning into a glide, floated on her back. The water was soft and soothing, her limbs loose and flexing. She all but dozed when a shrill cry rattled her teeth. A second later she heard: "Don't do it; you'll be cursed for life!" The voice was deep and harsh, and familiar. She splashed upright, and was immediately drawn to the hose — trained on Cash! Ann was fit to be tied; she swam to the edge and leapt out of the pool, the parrot squawking hysterically, trying to dodge the forceful stream.

Frantically she screamed, "AAAAUUUGGGHHH...!" The scream bounced off walls at triple the speed of sound. She sprinted up to Hoskins, all of one-hundred-and-three pounds laying into the caretaker, clawing and scratching and swinging wild, like *Catwoman* on uppers. "You're fired!" Big veins stood against her neck in cords, cheeks flashing to the color of new brick. "Get out! Get Out! GET OUT!"

THE CHIEF BUTLER NO SOONER GOT WIND OF IT WHEN HE phoned his boss. In detail, Rupert Bennett explained what had happened. Sparkle responded with complacency. "Tell Hoskins I appreciate the effort, but a little water is hardly enough to do the job."

"Yes sir, I'll tell him...but what about Ann? She's half-cocked!"

"Don't sweat it. Just spike her decaf and send her off to bed!"

* * *

ANN'S SUITE WAS SITUATED ON THE SECOND FLOOR clubhouse — just next to Cash's suite.

All the suites were the same — a standard-bearer for grace and hospitality, marble and crown molding throughout. A spectacular view of Sparkle Fairway stood just outside Ann's window, where a well-crafted landscape displayed rolling greens and intermittent stretches of water. A gold-leaf sunken tub sat center-room...mirrors everywhere. A switch panel filled the tub up with water, adjusted the climate, the lights, played music, and / or retracted the skylight for stargazing.

Upon drinking but a few sips of coffee, Ann got all drowsy, going straight to bed; she fell fast asleep, failing to draw the four-poster curtains.... She awoke in the dark after 11 hours sleep. She yawned and stretched and glanced up at the nightstand clock, which gave the time as 11:25 PM. She flicked on the lights, when John Phillips glimmered in the eye of her memory. She reached for the phone, and just then the door clicked open; Rupert Bennett entered with a tray the size of a manhole cover. He made for the coffee table, setting the tray down. The tuxedoed butler turned to Ann. "You've been asleep for quite a while, madam. I prepared a snack."

"How nice of you, Rupert... Appreciate it. So have you looked in on Cash?"

"Indeed, my lady. The bird is safe next door, dining on fresh bill-hook seeds."

"Thanks, Rupert; I could always count on you. You're a peach...!" Ann drew a compliment like a thug drew a pistol.

The butler creased a smile, clicked his heels, and bowed respectfully. "Please don't hesitate to call, madam." Rupert saw his way to the door, and thought: *The maid cleans the cage, feeds it...and I take all the credit. What a job!* The butler departed, closing the door behind him.

Ann reached for the phone, dialing the Long Distance Operator, placing a person-to-person call to John Phillips —

Somalia, Africa. She'd tried numerous times reaching him, but to no avail. This time, however, should prove successful, as 11.30 PM in Rosemont equated to 8:30 AM in East Africa. In order to satisfy a provision in the will, it was imperative she reach John.... Ann hit speakerphone, and got up. She sauntered up to the silver tray and scooped a handful of nuts, and returned to her bed. She sat on the edge nearest the phone, her leg folded under her; she chewed one nut at a time, salting her pink diaphanous *nightie*.... Finally she heard: "Your party is on the line..."

"Thanks Operator." The operator no more than signed off when someone began breathing heavily over the phone — deep, robust pants. "Hello, John...is that you?" Her eyes twisted.

"Hi, Ann...how's everything? *Whew...!* Excuse the heavy breathing. I was halfway to the bank of Muddy Rivers when the porter told me you were on hold. By the way, got your telegram..."

"You did, eh? When? It went out over a month ago!"

"Last week."

"Last week?"

"Sorry, Ann, but I've *been* on an expedition. I'm not always at the base camp!"

She heard animal sounds in the background, and got a reality check. "Okay, I understand, but you gotta believe me when I tell you we've got a lot riding on this!"

"I know we do!"

"Then why aren't you here? Look, if I could do this alone I would...but I can't! We gotta do this together! Jane's attorney made that perfectly clear."

"I know all about it! Listen, I'm just awaiting word...from the Zaire embassy in Washington. Once the visa comes back approved I'm as good as there."

"MOST DEFINITELY MR. SMITH.... FROM ROCKFORD TO NEW York is only a two day ride," said the man on the phone.

"Two days is okay, I guess. I just hate flying. So tell me, what *is* the fare?"

"Oh yes, the fare...." He cleared his throat: "*Ughmmmm...!* Quite reasonable, I assure you. Just four-hundred and forty-two dollars...tax included." A prickly silence came over the phone.... Mr. Smith, you still there? Mr. Smith, you read me? Oh Mr. Smith — MR. SMITH...!"

"I'm thinking it over."

"Oh...I see. So have you decided?"

"I'll walk."

"What, to New York...? Why, that's quite a distance!"

"That's *quite* a fare...! Okay, okay I'll pay it! At least it's cheaper than by air."

"Yes sir, indeed! And traveling by eighteen-wheeler is *much* safer...."

Once his travel plans were settled, he wrote in his journal:

> *There is one God, and one mediator between God and men: Christ Jesus. Since Jesus 'is' God, it follows that God exists in three persons: Father, Son, and Holy Spirit. Seeing as how Christ lives, the infernal Satan — the great enemy of humankind — too lives. In point of fact, all paranormal readings indicate spirits, good and evil, knocking at death's door.... Once the soul emerges from flesh, good and evil spirits will too emerge, and do battle for "that" soul — a sort of cosmic recruitment for the end times. However frightening the thought of death, eternal life is a simple matter of believing, as believing will empower God's angels to guard and protect. The disbeliever, however, will nullify all intervention, resulting*

*in damnation.... Of course, souls that teeter on the fence will be rejected from both worlds, and thusly trapped in earth's realm. Only in repentance will the entity enter the Kingdom.... To board the "heaven express" from the get-go, one must live by:*

## THE ETERNAL CODE*

The eccentric billionaire rearranged the alphabet, encrypting the Code:

Rsexbk-wxgpd uyxks pahynb hdpdoxdw nxup

*Break the Eternal Code and win cash prize — all contestants must be 18 years or older. See Website for details: www.CosmicDustCode.com.

132

## Chapter 21
## THE CONVENTION

HAYDEN PLANETARIUM
New York City
October 9th

T HEY CHECKED INTO MORTIMER, A FIVE-STAR HOTEL ON the corner of Central Park West and West 82nd Street. Each room was a suite, Mortimer a guest paradise, its mainstay elegance, Manhattan seen through large picture windows. Mary enjoyed the spa and all the pampering, Robert the free stay and all the savings, funded by NASA. Still, neither Robert nor Mary rated full comps, food paid for out of pocket.

LATE AT NIGHT, CENTRAL PARK WEST WAS FINALLY starting to flow, most people home in their soft beds, away from the cramped, somewhat claustrophobic quality of the Hayden Planetarium.

A plate glass window divided the planetarium with an outdoor observatory. The observatory was a force of technology, telescopes capturing every *nook* of the seeable galaxy. However, stargazing came with a price, as one minute of viewing costs one dollar.

The moon drifted behind a bank of clouds, casting shadows onto the heavens above. However dim the sky, people weren't deterred, lining up behind telescopes, hoping to see the rings of Saturn or the Face on Mars.

The planetarium was a beacon of solar mysteries, its main attraction the Hayden Sphere, which featured shows of unparalleled sophistication and excitement. Immediately across the way were the exhibits, where sales reps filled out orders on all the latest gadgets. Robert browsed the exhibits, studying a display entitled, *THE SEARCH FOR EXTRATERRESTRIAL INTELLIGENCE....* He unfolded his eyes on razor sharp nebula photos, and photos of far distant planets and galaxies. He wheeled to consider an exhibit on black holes, his glasses sliding down the bridge of his nose. He pushed up his glasses and settled his gaze on the Milky Way galaxy: magnetars flaring, gamma rays bursting.

A group of space-hounds left the Hayden Sphere, filing through turnstiles, meandering in all directions. Robert went about business, his curiosity crunching, glasses round and nerdy. Still, he looked sharp, his suit double-breasted, shoes polished to brilliance, and nicely groomed. Though dressed to the nines, he was still the same old Robert....

The same ol' cheapskate!

Robert's coattails pulled down in a tug, as someone tried to gain his attention; he turned, and saw no one. Suddenly a voice rang out from below — a rather shallow voice: "Mister, o' mister!" He glanced down, down to where a small boy was gazing up. The boy looked scared, and might have been lost.... "Yes, little boy, how may I help you...?"

"Mister, can I please have a dollar? Just one dollar...?"

Robert went white over his clammy skin, his jaw dropping, heart racing; sweat beaded his brow, plinking off the end of his nose.

"Mister, you okay?"

Powerless and paralyzed, Robert couldn't respond. Suddenly he blinked, as if dirt shot in his eyes. "Yes...I think so. Just dizzy! You were saying?"

"I'd really like to look into the telescope but it costs money...and I haven't any. Have you got a dollar, just one dollar?"

"Sure kid, I've got a dollar." The boy's face lit up like teaming star fields in the night. But then Robert added: "Sorry *kiddo,* I left it home."

The boy pouted, his lips pushing forward. Still, the tyke clung to his interests, determined to see into the telescope despite the odds against it — despite the man's stinginess. The boy turned, bumping into a woman with arm outstretched, extending him a dollar. The boy received it graciously. "Gee lady, you're swell!" He ran off to the observatory, the woman looking firmly at Robert. "You should be ashamed."

"Mary, you're looking wonderful!" He wrapped his arms around her, giving an embracing squeeze....

And all was forgiven.

THE PLANETARIUM HAD A SOUVENIR SHOP, WHICH provided magazines, beverages and light snacks.... Robert set bottled water down on the counter. He whipped out his wallet and turned to Mary. "Sure you don't want anything?"

"No, thank you, Robert; really, I'm fine."

The cashier rang up $4.99 and Robert handed in five dollars. "Sorry sir, I'm all out of pennies. Change is on the way, and will arrive within the hour."

"I'll wait."

Mary Evans was gifted at reading people. When she concentrated very hard she could interpret one's thoughts through the windows of one's eyes. Interpreting Robert, however, was like staring into a black hole. She nevertheless found him fascinating...in a naïve sort of way.

"Heard you left the company," he said.

"'Bout a month after you…"

"That soon, eh…? Where'd you go?"

"I moved to — " She hesitated, and then said: "Let's just say, the minute you went to Rockford I went to pieces!" Her face lit up, hoping he'd get it.

"Where…?"

She shrugged, and sighed audibly. "To Long Island… I'm renting a townhouse in Long Island."

"Oh, really…sounds nice. So whatever became of the team?"

"Still at Johnson…. And Mike was made team leader…!"

"Michael Bagley, team leader?" Robert raised his brow, and felt a sinking feeling.

"Know what you mean. Wasn't fair… I couldn't leave *fast* enough." She glanced over his shoulder, and spotted an old friend. "There's Major Penn!"

Robert turned, and saw the major on crutches at the Time Travel display. "Come on; let's say hi!"

They left the Souvenir Shop, and made a beeline for the major.

In his late thirties, Major Penn — attired in service dress — hobbled about the exhibits, caught up in the "bending space theory." Suddenly his name rang out from behind. He pivoted about, and saw two familiar faces, his head nodding in salutation. "Hi, Mary…Robert..how nice to see you…! So how's everything?" The major etched a smile.

"Can't complain," said Mary. "Just trying to stay busy and out of trouble."

"Have an accident?" said Robert, eyeing the crutches.

"No accident, just another space mission. My seventh! And they're getting longer each time…nine months, this last one."

"Nine months?" said Mary, somewhat dismayed.

"Microgravity will often result in calcium loss, and brittle bones. Re-entry into Earth's orbit was intense, pure torture, my metabolic structure struggling to re-adapt. My bones had all but turned to chalk, my Achilles' tendons stretched and throbbing. Especially my left foot! The ol' dogs just couldn't handle it."

"Sounds like 'The Agony of *Da-feet'!*" said Robert, taking a crack at witticism.

Mary gave Robert an odd, grimacing little smile. "Why, that's 'corn' that isn't even ripe yet!"

Major Penn chuckled. "Yes, well, gotta motor. Mustn't keep the colonel waiting! Good luck and Godspeed." The major turned, and walked haltingly toward the escalators.

Mary swiveled her head left, right, and all around, trying to take in everything at once: the shops, the things outside them, the displays, the people and their gawky expressions. Robert on the other hand was complacent, wrapped in his next seminar…his next conference meeting. "Listen," said Mary, looking at Robert, "I need to buy something. Wait here; only take a sec."

She headed for the Souvenir Shop.

## Chapter 22
## A WAR OF WORDS

A BAND OF SCIENTISTS APPEARED FROM OUT OF nowhere, stomping across the floor like Nazi storm troopers, their noses in the air. Michael Bagley led the charge, determined to lay into Robert, all gloomy and frown-like. He spotted Robert outside the Souvenir Shop, and headed his way.

Mike stopped before Robert, a redolence of salt wafting: Mike rode the high seas, and Robert, thrashing in tempest waters, was going down for the third time, waves of shock crashing over him. Mike felt great, gritting his teeth and working his jaw muscles as if chewing; he hummed with self-importance, and Robert, fading like an old photograph, couldn't suppress the enormous fear climbing up his throat.... Robert shifted his gaze to Clark and Alex, who stood smugly; Robert shriveled and shrank, like the Obama dollar. A second later he saw Rachel Gordon...a girl he once dated. "Rachel," he called out. Rachel turned, grimaced at Robert, and approached with foot-dragging reluctance.

"Hi Robert...what's up?"

Michael's face fell, his cohorts framed in wonderment.

"Gee Rachel, you put on a little weight."

"Yes Robert, I did. *Now* I'm seeing a guy who feeds me."

Mike smirked, and his boys snickered.

"Anyways," said Rachel…"gotta boogie. Catch'a on the flip side…!"

Rachel departed and Mary reappeared, nudging her way through Michael and company. She handed Robert a gift — a keychain with a heart-shaped ornament attached to it.

"For me…?" said Robert brightly. "You shouldn't have. I mean, it makes Mike look cheap."

Mike turned livid. "Me, cheap…? Sorry pal, I'm not you! I'm not the one with the zipper on his wallet that has yet to make its first zip…! Why, you live so close to your money even your skin is layered in it…!" He drew breath, and continued. "No *one* squeezes money like you…! You pinch a penny so tight both heads and tails come out on the same side of the coin!" Clark and Alex broke up laughing, and Mike, throwing out his chest, turned to Mary. "You're looking especially pretty tonight. What would I have to give you to steal a kiss?"

"Chloroform…!"

Michael stared at her briefly, and then let out a wild bark of laughter…. He fell silent, his face darkening, and turned to Robert. "Can't give a kid a buck, eh? You're nothing but a geek — a cheep geek!"

Robert sweated coldly, and Mary turned to Clark Foy. "Is that how *you* feel, Clark?"

Clark drew his shoulders up in a shrug, and offered no response.

She swiveled her gaze to Alex Peterson. "And where do *you* stand on all this?"

Alex likewise had nothing to say; he studied Mary's nose, taking a sudden interest in flared nostrils.

She addressed all three of them, saying, "Let's get something straight… Everything Robert's ever done was for the team. *Our team!* The Gold Team! What is your problem? Is it the Nobel?

'Cause if *that's* it, you're forgetting something. He earned it! And if *that* bothers you than you're the ones with the problem; not he...!"

"Yeah, right, like it's *my* problem!" said Mike, his tone gruff. "All Robert did was slip through the crack — that's all! He got lucky, nothing more. Who cares, anyway? So he got some exposure. Huh! Big whoop-dee-do! You want to compare brain pans? I won the 'Thomas Alva Edison award' at age seventeen."

"Oh, really...? Robert had graduated summa cum laude at sixteen."

The veins were starting to pound a war chant in Mike's head. "I was published when I was twenty."

"Wow, I'm impressed! Wanna learn something? Take a page from Robert's book... When Robert was twenty he'd written for *Quantum,* papers so classified even *he* wasn't permitted to read them!"

Mike thought he was going to have a brain hemorrhage. "I taught at Harvard for three years!"

"That's nothing, Robert taught at —" She paused, and rubbed her chin. "He taught at —" She turned to Robert. "Where *did* you teach?"

"Never taught school..."

"Ah-haa!" said Mike, wide-eyed and gloating. "Robert can't teach; his brain is too tense...*two-tenths* the size of a normal brain!" Clark and Alex broke up laughing.

Robert said to Mary, "Tell them about the Ray!"

"What's that? What's the Ray?"

"Don't know? Tell you later; let's just leave. You hungry...?"

"I'm starving!"

"I'm buying. Know this great little restaurant — Pete's Place makes the greatest hamburgers, and tipping isn't required. They even have a pinball machine. C'mon, we'll have the greatest time! Sky's the limit — money won't mean a thing."

Suddenly the cashier appeared from out of nowhere. He approached Robert with arm extended. "Excuse me sir, here's your *penny* change."

"Thanks" said the big spender, receiving the coin and slipping it into his pocket. Robert and Mary no sooner turned than Mike jumped in Robert's path, stopping him cold. "Not so fast, bub. You've got a debt to settle, and you're not leaving till you cough up."

Mary's heart froze, her blood running cold. Mike was up to his old tricks, and the odds were six-to-five Robert would slip into "auto-think." All Mike had to do was rattle Robert's cage and Robert would "auto-think": racing thoughts, confused speech, and incoherent ramblings.

Amazing he hadn't lost his driving privilege.

"You had no business using my computer!" Mike had said gruffly.

"What are you talking about? What computer?"

"You know what computer — don't act innocent!"

"Sorry Mike; don't know a thing about it."

"You know *everything* about it!"

Robert scratched his cheek, and suddenly it dawned on him. "Oh...you mean the one in the Mission Control Rec Hall."

"Yeah, that one...!"

"The desktop with the duel drives, high-speed internet and all-in-one printer."

"That's right!"

"The one with the tab key that sticks, and runs slow as molasses in January."

"I SAID YES! And I'm charging you a hundred bucks wear-and-tear... Call it a rental fee."

"But Mike, I never used it. Never even went near it!"

"Isn't that too bad, 'cause I'm charging you anyway."

"Huh?"

"That's right — one-hundred bucks pal! If you didn't use it, that's *no fault* of mine. *It* was there for you to use."

Robert twisted his eyes, and tried to follow Mike's logic; something about it almost made sense... "Now let's see if I've got this straight: You're charging me for something I didn't use because it's not your fault that I didn't use it. Is that it?"

"Quit stalling!"

Robert grinned, his dimples bracketing brightly. "I don't owe you a thing, Mike. We're even! C'mon Mary, let's go…"

"Stop," said Mike sharply. "No one's *going* anywhere!"

Robert froze.

"How do you figure?" asked Mike.

"You owe *me* a hundred dollars for kissing my girl, Mary. Call it a rental fee."

Mary's heart lurched, and didn't know where this was going.

"I *never* kissed Mary!" proclaimed Mike.

"Now isn't that too bad, 'cause I'm charging you anyway."

Mike opened his mouth, closed it again, opened it once more, shut it. He was apparently struggling to remember how to talk. Finally he croaked "Huh?"

"Just because you didn't kiss her is *no* fault of mine. 'It' was there for you to *use!"*

Mike's face clouded, and his fair-skinned cronies snickered. Mike spun into his flunkies: "Shut-it!" He turned back to Robert. "Don't hand me that!"

"I'm not handing you anything — particularly a hundred dollars."

"Oh yeah…? We'll see!"

"Listen Mike," Robert had said pointedly, "since I'm not about to *give way* and there's only *one way* — *your way* — let me put it *another way:* Mary and I are leaving *that way!"* Robert took Mary's hand and nodded at the escalators; he skirted around his former team, Mary by his side. Mike's blood ran cold, the two of them disappearing before his eyes. Mike started to gasp, his heartbeat throbbing…could almost hear the sweat oozing from his pours.

LARKIN'S JEWELRY HOUSE WAS HIGH-END, SITUATED IN THE heart of New York's business district. Late at night, Larkin's was in the throes of being robbed, the alarm rendered dysfunctional, cameras shielded in paint, guard bound and gagged.

Big Ed worked the backroom, Moose and Cody the showroom, scooping handfuls of diamonds from glass cabinets and shoving them into bags. George and Stanley presided over a pallet of black jeweler's felt, littered with bright gemstones, their stomachs pressing into the showcase.... Stanley spotted a stone of particular interest, and slipped on a monocle. He carefully examined the stone, and muttered, "Ah, emerald jade...carved in the fashion of the Ming dynasty. Jade rules...*really boss.* This rock *rocks...!*" George slapped him on the back of the head: "There's no time for that!"

"Okay! Okay!" He threw down the eyepiece and upended the pallet, pouring precious gems into a bag.

He pocketed the stone.

ROBERT AND MARY FELL INTO THE BACK OF A CAB, THE driver swinging around in his seat. "Where to...?"

Without skipping a beat, Mary said: "Fitzwilly's Gourmet!"

The driver hit the meter. "You got it!" He punched the gas and sped down the avenue.

Robert's eyes flashed gray before him. He rubbed his hands together, and realized he'd lost all feeling — except for his fingernails, which were extremely sensitive. His lips turned blue, and intense pain crept into his lower back and pelvic region. Something in the name, *Fitzwilly's,* didn't set well. Worse, *gourmet!* Tight in the throat, he looked for his voice. "Mary, please, I beg of you...anywhere but Fitzwilly's!"

"Why not 'Fitzwilly's'...?" She waited for a response but none was forthcoming. She saw him blinking back tears.... "Don't do this, Robert, because now I *want* to know. What's wrong with Fitzwilly's?"

"Everything...! I mean, what's *right* with it?"

"What's right with it? That's easy. For one, it's a New York landmark. Two, the doors are solid mahogany, adorned in thick and weighty brass. Three, the carpets and drapes are all hand-woven, and supremely costly. Four, the tables are ornately carved, replete with white linens and expensive silver tableware. Five, the pond and rock waterfall is a work of art, the décor absolutely —"

Robert past out, slumped over in his seat. "Robert, Robert, what happened — what's wrong with you?" Frantic, she slapped him.

His eyes flew open, but his mind remained closed, wondering around in blackness. He started talking crazy: "Cosmic dust indeed plays a role in the creation and formation of our —"

She grabbed hold of him, and shook.

He came around, his mind awake and aware. He took a deep breath, exhaled slowly, and hearkened back to the restaurant. "Right, Fitzwilly's...okay, I get it. But you're missing the point. Point is locals don't eat there! And if the locals won't eat there, c'mon, you *know* something's wrong."

"So what you're saying is locals don't eat there. Really...?"

"Really...ask any cabdriver...!" The cabbie didn't care to get involved, and minded his business. Robert continued. "There isn't one cabdriver in all of Manhattan who eats there. And do you know why?"

"Can't afford it?"

"Don't be silly; of course they *can* afford it! It's their gimmick. Fitzwilly has the most ridiculous gimmick!"

She hesitated...then said: "Okay, I'll bite. What is it? What's their gimmick?"

"You really want to know?"

"Yes, I want to know! What's *this* gimmick?"

Robert swallowed dryly. "Their servers...their waiters are the gimmick."

Mary dropped her jaw. "Waiters...?"

"Precisely... You see, Mary, all the waiters are little people — dwarves."

"Little people...? Dwarves...? Now why would they do that?"

"'Little people' make the steaks *look* bigger."

She gave him a deadpan stare, and folded her arms. "We're going to *Fitzwilly's!*"

144

## Chapter 23
## STICKER SHOCK

W HILE THE RESTAURANT DID NOTHING TO LIFT ROBERT'S spirits, Mary had enough *chutzpah* for the both of them.

They arrived at eleven pm, when *Fitzwilly's* was on the wane and tables plentiful. They headed straight for hatcheck, checking in garments before following the maitre d' through the piano lounge.... Mary sauntered with the grace of a ballerina, her frame slender and curvaceous, swaying to "Theme from Love Story." Robert gazed up at the piano-man, and noted his tux: The temperature rose and Robert broke a sweat — lavish restaurants had that effect on Robert...and cheapskates in general.... They entered a candlelight room, where a stone waterfall added illumination: Water trickled into the pond and good-luck coins sat at the bottom of it. Robert spied the coinage and rubbed his hands together, and smacked his lips.... They matched the headwaiter's stride, following him to a walled booth in back of the room. The headwaiter gestured the booth with a single wave of his hand: "A table for *two* earnestly longs for *you.*"

145

Mary slid into her seat and the maitre d' departed. She raised her gaze to Robert, who stood awkwardly beside the booth, fidgeting with a handkerchief. Suddenly a dollar spilled out of it, fluttering down to the tabletop. Robert's vision became increasingly clear, whisking the money back into the hanky and into his pocket. He loosened his tie, undid his upper button, and eased into the booth.... Mary opened her menu and Robert, picking up a place napkin, tapped his drippy nose and wet face with it. The aroma of richly sauced dishes filled the air, and Robert perused the white linen and crystal and silver tableware, his head reeling, heart all but stopping — like Superman and kryptonite.

He picked up his menu, and just then the waiter appeared from shadow. "Good evening; my name is Mark, and I'll be your waiter. Please look over our selection. I'll be back shortly to take your order." The waiter departed, and Robert gaped at Mark's poise — his perfect tux.

Mary closed the menu and draped her napkin over her lap. She took in the room's ambience and someone poured water into her glass.

Low conversation and the ping of cutlery against china hung in the air; Robert painstakingly studied the entrées.

The waiter was again upon them. "Would you like more time?"

"No, thank you; I think we're ready," said Robert, peering up and over his glasses at Mark. "Incidentally, have you got frog legs?"

"Gee, I hope not. I always walk this way."

Robert sat speechless. He folded his arms, and huffily said "Well!"

Mark pulled out his pad, and Robert said: "Being a simple man of simple tastes, I will naturally dispense with the appetizer."

Mark flinched at the emboldened remark....

Robert buried his face in the menu, and muttered: "Old World pasta, $28.95. Honey-fried chicken, $31.95.... Brisket of beef, *whoops!* Maine Lobster...*huh?* Filet Mignon — *OUCH...!*"

Robert said to Mark, "I'll have the Old World pasta."

Mary said, "Skip the *whoops!* hold the *huh?* and bring me the — *OUCH!* well-done...."

THE DOBERMAN PINSCHER LONGED FOR MASTER MOOSE, who so happened to be tied up at Larkin's!

The heist consisted of three cars: one, a Z06 Corvette, the other two, SRXs. The Cadillacs were black and identical, the Corvette sporty fast. Still, the Vette's windows were bulletproof and weighty, which hindered speed — as did George and Stanley, who drove it. Between them, they matched the weight of the car, windows and all. Small wonder they would rather use Stanley's roomy, comfy Lincoln. The Lincoln, however, wasn't conducive and, bottom line, George and Stanley were stuck with the 'Vette.

They had to make the most of it.

A cloud shifted, and moonlight overspread the alleyway. *Killer* (dog) — locked inside the Caddy — spotted them entering the Corvette; it cocked its head at George twisting and squeezing, Stanley pushing and shoving, the car teetering and flattening.

The plan was for George and Stanley to leave Larkin's two minutes before the others. Two minutes, Moose had figured, was time enough to send the NYPD on a wild-goose chase, for the 'Vette was a decoy. A diversion... A subterfuge....

BUS PEOPLE CLEARED AWAY DISHES, TIME CREEPING INTO the night.... They'd eaten their food in complete silence, except for the sounds of munching. Robert took a sip of black coffee, now approaching a drinkable temperature. He set his cup down, and gazed into Mary's eyes, wondering if everything was okay. Finally she said, "So what's it like in Rockford?"

"It's, uh...peaceful and quiet. But that's how I like it. Got a big home and nice laboratory...."

"Really...? What are you working on?"

"Oh, just stuff... Nothing that would interest you, I'm sure...." Robert studied her reaction, hoping he'd struck a nerve; he was the picture of a man glowing with anticipation.

"Well, I don't know. You're a pretty interesting fellow. Try me..."

"If you must know, I'm extracting cosmic dust from the Milky Way galaxy."

"Cosmic dust...? Why cosmic dust...?"

"CD holds —" he began.

"CD...? Oh...*cosmic dust.* Go on; I'm listening."

"CD holds clues of life as we know it. CD is a derivative of star matter and life is composed of elements of stars. CD is a forerunner, the precursor of life — the quintessence of all living things."

"Oh, really...? But Robert, the Milky Way is tens of thousands of light-years away. How do you expect to get there?"

"I don't have to reach the Milky Way intrinsically, you understand. Any dust cloud along the way will suffice."

"But still —" she started. "Okay, let's suppose you find a way at this 'cloud,' what then? How do you deliver it?"

"It's covered! For one, I've got enough gadgetry to choke a horse. Secondly, it's already been tested. It works! As for *how* it works — well — there really isn't time for all that."

She stared at him blankly. "Skip the details, what are these 'gadgets' you speak of?"

"Oh, you know, the usual stuff: high-powered laser, optical telescope, magnetometers, thermo cameras, psychographs, frequency counters, EMF detectors, EVP record —"

"Stop...!"

"Huh?"

"Robert, psychographs are used to chart personality traits..."

"Yes, they certainly do. They also play a roll in spirit photography."

"Really...? She rubbed her delicate chin and gave the matter thought. "I see — well then — it adds up."

"What adds up?"

"The magnetometers, the EMF detectors and the like...those things are associated with ghost activity — detecting ghosts...! What're you, some kinda Doctor Frankenstein?"

"Yes, most definitely…. I mean, NO…! Just wish you were there to offer an assist. The results will be staggering!"

"Ah-huh…I'll bet." Mary creased a distant smile, and reached out to his arm, like throwing a life preserver. Her eyes were dry, strained with the knowledge that this was not the way things worked. "Robert, CD may well explain how the solar system was formed but that's as far as it goes. As for anything else — 'the quintessence of all living things' — I think not. You can't equate life to CD without proof. Your theory is absent of evidence."

"I beg to differ…absence of evidence is *not* evidence of absence. And besides, I already did it."

"Did it? Did what?" She pulled back her hand.

"Extract CD from the galaxy. Did you know cosmic dust is transparent? That is until it reaches earth's orbit, when great splendor blossoms into beautiful orbs, orbs that could quite possibly be life itself. My only quagmire is — well — its downside."

"Downside…?"

"Right…because the minute one becomes absorbed, angels and demons will emerge onto the psychograph screen. The screen showed images of glorious angels doing battle with an array of creatures, the likes of which never imagined. Both upper and lower worlds were in conflict, a battle of enormous magnitude. The demons were hideous and grotesque, all shooting flames from their mouths, eyes red and fiery, wingspans wide and far reaching, tails long and serrated. Some had hoofed feet and sharp horns while others had two heads and satyr-like features. Completely and utterly macabre…."

"You don't say…"

"I *do* say…!" He fell silent for a second, and turned despondent. "I just never expected the dark side of paradise. I was taken aback, and for the first time I read the Bible…and for the first time things became clear. Namely, the "key to heaven"!

Her eyes twisted. "The key to heaven…?"

"The Eternal Code…"

"What's that, the Eternal Code?"

"It's a lot of things, but in a nutshell it's God's pathway to heaven."

"Sounds interesting…"

"That's not all!"

"It's not?"

"Suddenly disaster struck, an inexplicable meltdown erasing all evidence! Completely gone, as if some "thing," some power beyond my control were preventing me from all this. Sparks and flares shot everywhere, when I grabbed the extinguisher and sprayed down my equipment. Thick smoke hung in the air, and all the angels and demons had vanished, wiped out of existence!"

It wasn't good, Robert getting excited like this. She had hoped their conversation would peter out, but rather than run aground Robert got overly heated, the dimly lit room suddenly bright, sounds abnormally altered and distorted, as if the room's ether had dissipated. Her mere presence stirred Robert's passions, and Mary feared "auto-think".… She got up and slipped into shadow, hoping to avoid disaster.

Robert's head pounded…mouth stale and dry. He bent over and stuck his hands between his knees, his thoughts racing. He gazed into his coffee cup and teetered back and forth, shrieking in pain. He covered his ears, blocking out the phantom voices from within. Who knew what deep seeded problem laid waiting in his subconscious, ready to lash out at the first sign of weakness? On the verge of "auto-think," Robert wandered around in darkness, looking for light.

He sat up in his seat, his eyes pinned wide, his breathing quick and shallow.

Suddenly it hit him.

*BAM!*

Off to see the wizard.


*THE HUMAN MIND IS OFTEN FLAMED WITH STRANGE complexes.*

A middle-aged man in a brown suit approached Robert, alone at the booth. The man's heart raced and his temples pounded, a woman by his side. Robert raised his gaze, and barely made out the man's presence — the glower beating down at him. Like an evil wind, the man's breath was airy and rattling, his cell phone on the fritz, watch haywire. The woman by his side didn't own a watch, and nor was she the wife. The little woman (his wife) had threatened to clobber him if he got home one second past twelve...! He needed the time but fast....

"Hey buddy, *quick!* what time is it?"

"Time...? As in Eastern, Central, Pacific...?" Robert spoke fast and feverish.

"Huh? Yeah! What's the time?"

"Ah yes, time, the system in which two identical events are distinguished by various intervals of the Earth and motion thereof, all of which is orchestrated by the solar system with respect to planets and stars and, most indubitably, the theory of —"

"Come again?" The man froze in gaping astonishment, and Robert, his gaze blank, struggled with the psychotic stranger from within, trying to overtake his brain. Still, before the man knew which end was up, Robert continued: "Since time is vital to everyday life, I suggest we start at the beginning; that is to say, the sun, and how it relates to —"

"Stop!" the man finally said. "I ask for the time and you tell me how to build a clock! What're you, sniffing glue? Look pal, you've got a watch and I need the time! Don't have to be a 'rocket scientist' for that!"

A young man in a tailored gray suit appeared from nowhere, edging his way through "Timeless" and the woman. The young man presented Robert pen and paper, his face yearning. "Please, sir, may I have your autograph?"

Robert shook his head, kick-starting his brain back into motion. He blinked his eyes, slowed his breathing, and melded into a state of calm. He took possession of the pen and paper. "You certainly may." He jotted down his name and the timeless man stood in gaping wonderment. "Timeless" whirled into the gray suited man. "Now why on earth would you want *this* clown's autograph? He's nuttier than a fruitcake!"

"But that's Robert Smith."

151

"Oh, really…? What of it?"

"Nobel laureate…famous 'rocket scientist.'"

The man's face fell, his body frozen. A second later, threw out his arms in outrage. He took his lady friend's hand and, rolling his eyes to the back of his head, left in a huff. The young man shook Robert's hand, and he too departed…. Mary returned not a moment later. She slid back into the booth and gazed into Robert's eyes, those *once* wayward eyes, and saw sparks of awareness. She noted his clammy skin and soaked shirt, and realized just *how* worked up he'd become.

Mark was again upon them. "Would you care for dessert? Our ice cream is *sure* to whet your appetite…"

"Ice Cream?" exclaimed Robert. "Ice cream reduces enzymes in the lower esophagus. Or didn't you know that?" Mary blinked, as if she'd been slapped.

"No sir, I *didn't* know that."

Robert shook his head, tsk-tsk, expressing his displeasure. "And is your ice cream wet and mushy or firm and cold…? Probably all wet and mushy…!"

"Not at all, sir…our ice cream is firm and cold — extremely cold!"

"Extremely cold, huh…? So it's okay that I should get 'sphenopalatine gangleoneuralgia,' is that it?"

"Huh?"

*"Brain freeze…!"*"

"Why, no…!"

"Frankly, Mark, you should know better…. I sincerely hope you're not hitting the bottle."

"I should say not!"

Mary felt a sudden twinge of unease, her cheekbones flashing pink. She gaped wide-eyed, as if one of the walls had grown lips and started to talk. Robert's sudden bout was alarming, and Mary couldn't make sense of it. Maybe he was trying to be funny or maybe he hadn't yet recovered. Or maybe he *had* recovered but was having aftershocks, like an earthquake.

She looked despondently up at Mark. "No, thank you…I'll do

without."

The waiter set down the check. "I'll take this when you're ready." He then departed.

Silence ensued, and Mary thought of Robert's stinginess. She couldn't fathom him paying the tab. Not even a fraction. To avert further incidence, she said, "I've got this," and picked up the leather folder.

"Okay" was Robert's only reply.

She opened the folder, and Robert said: "I'll spring for the tip." Mary was beside herself, and didn't know what to make of it — nor did she refuse the offer.

Robert reached inside his coat neither slowly nor quickly, almost routinely, and removed a bill from a concealed pocket. Mary gazed at the bill's denomination and swore it was a *hundred!* But that was preposterous; Robert would never leave such a tip. Nevertheless, she placed her money inside the folder and waited for Robert to include the gratuity. But before he did, he waggled a finger, calling Mark over.

Mark approached with dignity. "Yes sir, how may I help you?"

"Just a little something for our esteem and appreciation…the service was most delightful."

"Thank you, sir; we do our humble best."

Robert revealed the greenback — a c-note…! A shadow crossed Mary's face, her thoughts upside down. Robert flaunted the money and Mary sat in gaping silence. She saw him fold the bill into his right palm, extending his hand to Mark, shaking Mark's paw. Mark beamed with delight, and Robert took back his hand, leaving a "hundred dollars" inside Mark's clutch.

Robert and Mary got up and ambled toward the exit…. They no sooner departed than Mark opened his hand, and saw he'd been duped.

Somehow he was holding a piece of paper that read: *"Tip" of the day: Stay drunk and prevent hangover.*

## Chapter 24
## CAUGHT IN THE MIDDLE

THICK FOG BLANKETED MANHATTANN, HAUNTS AND frights lurking in shadow, Halloween arriving early — the 10<sup>th</sup> of October. Despite the eeriness, Robert suggested a walk back to the hotel. "C'mon," he said, "the walk will do us good!"

"Well, okay…guess it won't hurt." She was hardly surprised he should want to save a buck.

They headed south on Amsterdam, arms swinging, hearts pumping, the avenue rather busy for the A.M.… Mary raised her gaze to the pay-no-attention-to-the-arrows crowd up ahead, and pushed in that direction…. When they reached the intersection a long truck jockeyed into West 86<sup>th</sup> Street, and blocked traffic. The truck hitched back and forth and pedestrians stalled, bumping into each other. Robert pulled his collar about his ears and rubbed his gloved hands together, and waited patiently. Mary, however, wasn't so patient, latching onto his hand. "C'mon…let's go look for a cab."

He didn't bicker, and strolled along…. Pumped-up, Mary

drew out and Robert dawdled behind, his legs straining, lungs churning. She slowed her pace and Robert caught up, city-lights breaking in the branches of overhanging trees.... She stopped suddenly, at an alleyway between West 87th and West 88th Streets. She turned to him, a low-key smile creasing her face. "Forget the cab; I know a shortcut." She pulled him into the alley and continued on, the atmosphere dark and foggy, warehouses muffling their footsteps. With their hands clasped, she tried not to get ahead of herself, Robert all jittery, afraid of shadows.... Something scurried by, the low-hanging fog parting. He stopped suddenly, and snapped back his hand. "What's that?"

"What, you scared? A mouse, an itty-bitty mouse..."

"No way...! If that's a mouse, the rats are kangaroos! Let's get a cab. I don't like alleys!"

"Don't be silly, we're almost there. You can do this! C'mon, I'll hold your hand."

Robert surrendered his paw and continued on.

A high-pitched squeal rang out, stopping them cold. They looked up, and saw *two* cars barreling in from Broadway, jetting towards them. They spun around, and two more cars thundered in from the opposite end, headlights framing them in the alleyway. Two cars at either end rocketed toward the middle, forcing them alongside a Dumpster, out of harm's way.

Four cars ground to a stop — all men in black, all sporting guns. She hauled Robert behind the Dumpster, which stunk to high heaven, flies dropping like flies. Still, had to make the most of it....

"Pull around!" snapped Moose.

"I can't! We're hemmed!" said David Siegel, driver.

Moose's two cars were caught in the middle, trapped by two other cars — two hostile cars. Moose felt oddly separate from his men, as if he and Sparkle were in this alone. He wondered if he might not just lose his head and start cursing everyone out. Time rushed by in spurts, and Moose, squirming in his seat, was all but a basket-case.... He suddenly remembered his insurance policy — Killer — calming things down. But the dog was nowhere in sight, and in all likelihood was out gallivanting with George and Stanley.

Moose studied the opposition, when doors flung wide and Sparkle's boys all ran for cover. He spotted Ace Flint, and cringed at Ace's gun skills: Ace was a dead shot, best trigger-man in the biz, and Sparkle had the cutting edge.... Moose buzzed down his window, and yelled out in a throaty, take-no-gruff voice: "Let's not be rash...we can work this out. Lose the *roscoes!*"

"Okay, fine...but no funny business or you won't see the light of day," shouted Ron Levy, a Sparkle confederate.

Moose and David Siegel (driver) slid out of the car — the other car the same, as Cody Walker and Big Ed Malloy stepped out into view. They stood beside their respective cars, watching as Sparkle's boys closed in, holstering their guns. George and Stanley whizzed across Moose's mind. He muttered, "Never around when you need 'em...!" He joggled his head, and harkened back to the moment...and realized Sparkle wasn't with his boys. His internal defenses flared, his head aching — a steady throb in both temples. He turned to Ace. "Where's *Dirty Bird?*"

"Who's *'Dirty Bird'?*"

Moose shifted his eyes side to side, as if a fly was buzzing all around his nose.

The Dumpster smelled awful, like putrid eggs and ripe cheese. Robert removed a handkerchief to filter out his nose, his blood curdling. But just as the hanky unraveled a dollar spilled out of it, fluttering to the ground! Robert let out a biting *"YIKES...!"*

Heads swerved into the Dumpster, and Ace ordered Crack to check it out.

Meanwhile, Sparkle flexed his knees on a nearby roof, all but ready to pounce on Moose when the *"YIKES"* stopped his forward motion. He scanned the below area, zeroing in on the two trash-bin people.

Mary cringed at their blown cover.

The *hophead* was soon upon them, armed and dangerous. "Okay, party's over — out!" Crack's eyes were red and glazed, but his frown was commanding. Still, his .45 wavered left to right, high and low, and could go off if only by accident.

156

They played it safe and got out.

Sparkle hit the pavement with hardly a jolt, landing just yards away. He burst up to the strange man and woman, who stood open-mouthed at his relaxed carriage, his fiery eyes, his dark and swarthy countenance; he checked his stride in front of them.

Crack immediately started back for the car.

"Stop...!" Sparkle snapped.

Crack ground to a halt, and swiveled about. "Huh?"

"Get back here, and keep an eye on these two!"

"Want me to take 'em for a ride, Boss?"

"When I get through with Moose we'll all take 'em for a ride...a one-way ride up the Hudson!"

Robert gulped dryly, his complexion draining color. "Don't wanna be rude or anything, but I can't swim! Water thrashing will invariably affect a threshold of drowning."

Sparkle looked him dead in the face, and said nothing.

"Hear what I said? I can't swim!"

"Don't sweat it — the 'dead' don't have to." Sparkle looked suspiciously sinister.

Robert turned pale white. "B-but my future...what about my *future...?*"

"*Past...!* All you've got now is a *past,* bub...!"

"Past...?" Robert squeaked. "I don't want to die...please, spare me...! Listen, I've got plenty of money. Release us and I'll make it worth your while. I'll pay each of you — " Robert thought about it.

Sparkle smirked condescendingly. He turned, and strutted away.

"Nine dollars...!"

Sparkle leaned back, arms swinging at an even gate, body erect and unhurried. The swagger was down cold.

"Ten dollars...!"

Mary whirled into Robert, her eyes two slits. "Why? Why did you *'yike'?"*

Robert gave an exaggerated shrug. "Couldn't help it...saw a dollar and got excited."

Mary rolled her eyes, her mouth bobbing but saying nothing. She shook her head side to side, and emitted a deep groaning sound: "Uggghhhh!" like Lurch on the *Addams Family* show.

Sparkle dug in his heels, and Moose morphed into the look of death. Just then his men, his judgmental men, tumbled through his head. He brought out his chest and sucked in his gut, those green eyes glowing.

Sparkle raised his gaze to Moose. "Be smart and surrender the stones."

"If I don't...?" Moose was starting to gather confidence.

"What're you, stupid? Your mouth is as big as a basketball and twice as empty. If you don't, you'll ascertain the taste of your liver!"

Moose gulped, his head throbbing like a bad tooth. Sparkle had the dueling edge, and Moose — trying to ignore his pulsing temples — capitulated. "They're in the trunk."

Sparkle turned to Al, and nodded at his DTS. "Pull it back."

Al responded sharply, falling in behind the wheel and backing up.... Once the car cleared, Sparkle moved in behind the STS.

Following the soft click, the trunk-lid rose and the jewels inside started to growl menacingly. Sparkle's arms shot up, his knees flexing, vying for position.

"Killer"!

*Mano a Mano a Dogo!*

Moose folded his arms across his full arched chest, his headache completely gone.... He approached the trunk, and gained the Doberman's attention, pointing a digit at Sparkle; Killer raised its upper lip and snarled like a wolf from the wild. Moose no sooner commanded "kill" than the dog flashed its fangs and sped forward, foam splattering in curds. Sparkle remained perfectly still when, to everyone's amazement, two knife hands appeared from out of nowhere, chopping the dog clear across the neck; Killer hit the pavement in a dull thud, thrashing about before drawing up its legs and lying still on the cold, damp ground. Simmering tensions hung in the air, when Killer got up, whimpered, and leapt back inside the trunk.

A mounting horror befell onlookers, giving Mary opportunity to scan the area; she checked out a gate just before a warehouse, which appeared ajar. She heaved a sigh.

Moose was meanwhile breathing convulsively, the pain in his head a real banger. He poked his head inside the trunk, panic fogging his brain. "Get out here and do your job, why don't you? Kill! Kill! Kill!"

The dog lay utterly still, having *none* of it.

Sparkle whipped out a pocket mirror and comb and fixed his hair, fluttering in the wind.

Crack stood in stupefaction, his .45 dangling by his side. He suddenly snapped up his gun, and waved it sporadically. "Don't know what you're thinkin' but forget about it! 'Cause when this is *over* you're *over!* Up the river without a paddle, if you know what I mean…!"

Robert began to bawl and leak tears. He spoke in short, shallow gasps: "B-but I…don't even…like water!"

"Shut up! You'll get used to *it!*

## Chapter 25
## THE GREAT ESCAPE

*L*IKE WATER, SLUSH, AND CORNMEAL MUSH, MOOSE MORAN *was oozing gush.*

Whatever else could be said about Raymond Frederick Moran, the man was no lightweight. At six-feet-seven, Moose was a wall of intimidation, topping scales at three-eighty. He had indomitable courage, his limbs snaking muscles. His eyes were cold and piercing, like a $CO_2$ laser. He was like cheap booze — unsettling... With broad shoulders and a barrel chest, Moose — until now — could spar with the best of them.

Until now....

Though the air was chilled the heat was on, and Moose couldn't stop sweat-beads from trickling down his spine. The jewels probed too close to the nerve, and wasn't about to throw in the towel.... He shimmied out of his topcoat and tossed it to Big Ed, henchman.

"Feelin' lucky, eh?" said Sparkle, edging closer. He *had* to lay it on thick or be left holding the bag — with nothing in it.

Sparkle lurched upward, his hands clutching Moose's collar, Moose's face turning blue. Moose tried to breakaway but the hands were deadly, like claws latching onto prey. His boys rushed in to break it up when Ace went for his gun, and everyone backed off; Ace withdrew empty-handed. Moose's men looked on in horror, powerless to act...apart from clamoring and shouting "dirty bird."

Moose was gasping, his vision blurred, barely able to make out Sparkle's eyes, that homicidal gleam; that *lethal* curl of the lip. Somehow Moose thought of breakfast — just one last breakfast with George and Stanley. But with Sparkle's cold breath filling his lungs, drowning him, food slipped further into nothingness. Sparkle's hands seemed to be carved from stone, and Moose, taking everything he had in him, couldn't muster the strength to cut loose. As a last-ditch effort he reflected on anger, countless days of anger, filling his every fiber with fury; he rolled all that anger into one ball of rage and slammed his knee into Sparkle's stomach like a battering ram. Sparkle let out a high-pitched yelp and released his grip, stabbing pains throughout his abdomen. But despite the hurt, Sparkle hit the pavement fast and furious, grabbing hold of two size fourteens and pulling forward, Moose flinging backwards, his head clipping the car going down. Moose landed flat on his backside and Sparkle, jumping down on Moose's torso, launched into a hail of punches, rearranging Moose's face. All the while, dense fog consumed visibility and the pounding — heard but not seen — was a nail biter, Moose flat on his back pleading between blows. Still, amid the cries, Sparkle wouldn't stop his assault and laid it on thick.

"Stop...! They're yours!" shouted Moose.

The blows ended and Sparkle got back up on his feet. "Get up, you big lummox! I said, get up!" He hauled Moose up by his collar.

"You can have the lousy ice," Moose blurted, blood running down his face. He blundered to the trunk of his car, and saw Killer all curled up in a dark corner. "Coward!" he hissed. Moose removed the leather bag and turned, when Sparkle started in his direction. Just then David Siegel wandered aimlessly forward, his jacket unzipped. Siegel's coat flapped in the wind, almost *flaunting* the .357 cradled in his shoulder holster; Moose spotted the rod and smacked his lips, lunging into Siegel and yanking out the gun; he aimed dead-on at Sparkle, coming at him. His finger on a hair trigger, said, "Do it, please do it — quench my thirst!"

"Go on and shoot, you can't hurt me!"

Moose fired, the shot sending chills up and down spines.

Crack looked on in a stupor, his knees buckling, all the breath going out of his body. Mary took it as a given, latching onto Robert's glove hand and practically dragging him down the alley; Robert bawled and wailed and ran clumsily behind. They ran toward a warehouse, the gate next to it ajar; Mary's purse flapped against her gyrations, and Robert, drenched in perspiration, couldn't stop his glasses from bouncing and sliding down his nose. She flung open the gate and hauled Robert inside, both running across the grounds — Tsang's Chinese Laundry.... A rim-shot rang out when Mary stumbled, her spike heel breaking off; she toed off her shoes and continued on in nylon stocking feet.

Meanwhile, Sparkle marched defiantly forward, and was no doubt sporting a bulletproof vest. Moose wasn't taking chances, elevating his gun for the eyes — right between the eyes. He gave fair warning: "Stop...or you'll get a three-fifty-seven caliber nose job...!" A second later the gun went off.

## *ChaBANGGG...!*

Sparkle's boys pitched back, the blast rattling bones and knocking teeth loose. But then suddenly, and simultaneously, they all went "Huh?"

Sparkle hadn't been grazed much less shot.

Moose angrily threw down the gun and latched onto David Siegel, his mouth a hair's breadth away; he spoke through extremely clenched teeth: "Ratted me out, huh? Why'd you do it? Who are you? Why'd you dime on me? You're getting burned for this! Hear me? Burned...!" His voice shook with intensity.

Sparkle threw his leg high into the air, ramming his foot into

Moose's shoulder, plunging Moose into the STS. Still clasping the bag, Moose's back was to the wall — or rather, the car.... He held out the bag in a gesture of forfeiture — weak, powerless, and ashen-faced. Sparkle snatched it away, and spoke in tones of a deranged psychopath: "Knew we could work it out." He turned, and strutted away when the D.B. name rang out from behind. Sparkle stopped abruptly, and set the bag down. His face masked in a scowl, wheeled about and burst up to Moose, who reiterated his sentiments. "You're nothing but a Dirty Bird...a filthy, Dirty —"

Sparkle plowed a balled-up fist into the big guy's solar plexus, sending the air out of billowing lungs with a single whoosh. Moose crumpled, wheezing as if congested. Moments later a blow landed squarely in his jaw, a well-placed uppercut crashing like a chugging locomotive into the chin. A haymaker! The knockout punch long overdue!

ALL THEY EVER WANTED WAS TO MAKE A CONTRIBUTION. Something, anything, just as long as it improved the quality of life as we know it.

The room was deadly quiet, the night reaching such a depth that every tiny movement seemed magnified. Robert sat rigid in shock so deep and so blue it felt cold as ice. Panic had a hold so complete he was unable to function in any way. If only he could get a grip. But with his heart slamming into his chest and the veins in each temple hollow pulsing angrily, moving mountains was easier. He pondered his doctor's counsel on stress management, closing his eyes and relaxing all major muscle groups, putting everything out of his head. But the images were too clear, the shock too deep. He opened his eyes and, for no apparent reason, went back to his youth: age seven, when three bullies had threatened to rough him up for money: one quarter each. He gave into their demands but not without incident: his breath stopped dead in his lungs, his nervous system shutting down, his heart stopping in the very act of beating. He was never sorrier for paying out *all* that money. Still, it took twenty-eight years to

Richard A. White

finally realize that life was worth more than 75 cents.

They sat in their own little areas, the room icy gray, their gazes hollow; they tried to hash things over but nothing made any sense. She drummed her fingers on the tabletop, the clicks deafening…. The finger tapping stopped when she reached up and pulled the chain, and turned on the ceiling light. She got up and joined Robert on the sofa. She sat at the opposite end, Robert glum and dejected, sitting low in his seat; she began to sidle near him. Soon they were knee-to-knee. She gave him an appraising glance, his hair haggard, his eyes puffy, face dingy. He was in *no* mood for conversation. She poked him with her elbow. "How ya doin', handsome…?"

He just stared at the coffee table, all depressed. "Sorry I was such a coward. If not for you we'd both be doing the backstroke right about now." A long sigh hissed through his teeth, his dimples pulling downward.

"At least you get to leave. How'd you like to live here?"

"No thanks!"

"Can't say I blame you… As for me — well — I'm in a pickle." She somehow assumed that all those men were from the New York area. "Those guys can spot me anywhere! But what can I do? I'm too old to cry and it hurts too much to laugh." A choking fear climbed up her throat, as if someone were hiding behind the TV.

Robert too was scared, trying to put it out of his mind. But it was just a bit much, and there wasn't enough space in his head for anything else…. He sat up in his seat and suddenly things turned bright, his blue eyes twinkling. "Come *stay* with me…at least until things cool down. I've got a big home and plenty of rooms. You'll be out of New York and out of danger. You can help me with my research!"

"Sounds nice, but I'll have to think about it."

"What's to think about? Every second you spend here increases risk. Those guys can spot you anywhere! C'mon…live a little! I'll introduce you to Dexter, my groundskeeper; great guy. You'll meet Grace the Maid…fabulous woman!"

164

An odd unrest settled over her, when a sense of glorious relief filled her being. "You know, I think you're right. I'll do it!"

*So what if Sparkle should hail from Illinois? What they don't know won't hurt them.*

"Great!" Robert raised his gaze to the dresser clock, and got up; he moved to the door, and opened it. Before leaving, he turned to her. "It's just past three... I'll go to my room and catch some shuteye, and in eight hours —"

"What's the hurry? We got all the time in the world!"

"But Mary, you gotta go home and pack and I've got to —"

"— relax!" she put in. "You've really got to relax!" "Did I ever tell you about my stepfather, my alcoholic stepfather?"

"Huh? No, I don't think so."

Robert never thought to ask about her past.

"All my life I've been pushed around, yelled at, and put down. Let me tell you, it was no picnic."

"Sounds awful...but Mary, I know the feeling..."

"Oh, really...? I don't think so."

"No, really; I do! When I was a boy my father *beat* me."

"Your father beat you?"

"My mother *beat* me too."

"YOUR PARENTS BEAT YOU?"

*"Chess...!* I let them *beat* me at chess."

Her eyes narrowed, and moaned painfully. She shook off his remark and pressed on: "Finally I land a job at NASA, and who do I have the pleasure of working with...Michael Bagley, who else? Like things weren't bad enough. Almost have to wonder what else can go wrong. But wonder no more, 'cause now I've got the mob on my back."

"What's your point?"

"Point is I rarely get to spend time with someone like you...someone with whom I can be myself. I'm scared, just little scared. And besides, if I wanted to spend another day alone I never would have taken you up on your offer." She elevated her voice: "Now, get in here!"

Robert stepped back into the room and closed the door. She

pulled him close to her. "Get closer, get closer!"

"If I get any closer I'll be standing behind you!" He put his arms around her and gave a hug. "Know just how you feel...I get the same way every time the IRS does an audit."

HAVING TAKEN ROBERT UP ON HIS OFFER, MARY ARRANGED for a moving van. Later that afternoon, she cleaned out her refrigerator and, in the event things didn't workout, rode out her lease, which wasn't up for another few months. They next loaded up her effects and took off for Illinois; they left New York effectively and expeditiously.

Upon settling in, she went right to work, maintaining records and helping in any and every way possible.... Despite all the craziness, Robert was the light of her life — the copious sun that rose and set around her feeble existence.

THE LAST THING THEY NEEDED WAS SOME ROUTINE TRAFFIC stop! They all wore seatbelts and drove well within the limit, two black Cadillacs streaming through the Lincoln Tunnel; they whooped and howled, like a college football victory.

Ron Levy drove the lead car, en route to Illinois. Crack sat opposite Ron, Sparkle the backseat, ignoring the hoopla; he studied his reflection in his pocket mirror...the powder residue on his face. Crack spun around in his seat to high-five David Siegel, who sat next to Sparkle. Ron shoved a fat cigar into the right side of his mouth, lighting it up; he exited the tunnel at a safe speed, keeping a safe distance from the car ahead.

The noise finally ended.

Sparkle said, "What happened?"

Ron pinned his eyes to the rearview mirror, and heaved a sigh.

Crack wheeled about in his seat, and fronted the deadly glare glued to him. "You mean those two people?"

A deafening silence ensued, when Sparkle roared, "What do you think I mean?"

Ron puffed nervously, gray smoke clinging to everything.

"Sorry, Boss, it *was* my fault. Let down my guard. You see, when Moose blasted you I thought he *really* blasted you! I got sick, really sick…and that's when they got away!"

Sparkle sighed gruffly; he rubbed a hand up and down the back of his neck. "Okay…guess maybe you're right."

"I am?"

"Shoulda told you guys Siegel's *gat* was filled with blanks. I'll take the hit on this one. Just the same, when we get back I'm sending out composite sketches to all my contacts. I aim to be as close to them as their conscience. Those two boneheads ain't gettin' away. They're dead meat!" A heavy load was lifted from Crack's shoulders, sinking calmly in his seat.

Sparkle threw out his paw. Siegel took it, the both of them shaking hands. "Sorry to see you go."

"Go? But, uh, where am I going?"

"Ruby's takin' over the Miami branch and you're moving to Vegas."

"What, another sting?" Siegel pulled back his hand.

"No sting…you're replacing Ruby as Head Honcho."

"Aw-right…! Ooo-weee!" Siegel slammed his fist into an open palm. "Always wanted to be Big Gun in Vegas…!"

## EPILOGUE

E<small>AST</small> A<small>FRICA WAS AN IMPENETRABLE CARPET OF GREEN</small>, the land fertile and dense, comprising of large plants and concealing large animal species. The geography was stunning and scenic, mosquitoes the size of vampire bats, raindrops the size of golf balls.

It rained all afternoon, falling in great drenching sheets, hammering the corrugated roof of the clinic in Jamame. The power went on and off throughout the storm, and wasn't until midday before the rain finally ceased.

John Phillips got a clean bill of health from the village doctor, leaving the East Clinic a foot taller. He strutted along the thoroughfare, and bumped into Tommy Arnold — a red-haired man in a hunter's hat and light beige khakis and suede boots. At age 22, Tommy had spent his youth learning the land, the wildlife, and the peoples of Eastern Africa; John Phillips was his mentor.

John extended his hand. Tommy took it. John had a firm, no-nonsense handshake. "Just want you to know, Tommy, today's your lucky day…"

"Come again?"

"You are now the proud owner of all my equipment…knives, guns, automatic feeders, hunting vehicles — the works! Just say the word, Tommy, and it's yours." John gave the ruddy-faced man back his hand and produced a list, an itemized list, handing it to Tommy; Tommy perused the list in jaw-dropping awe. "B-but John, I can't afford any of *this!*"

"Afford? Who's selling? It's yours, all yours, free and clear. Just drive me to Galkacyo International, and I'll sign over the vehicle registrations. My plane leaves in just under four hours."

"Sure thing John, you got it! When you wanna go?"

"I'm all packed and the Rover's loaded. Ready when you are."

"Great, let's do it…!"

John rode to the airport in complete silence, the road bumpy and uneven. The vehicle wasn't the most comfortable, and John, bouncing all around in his seat, chewed on his thoughts, wondering if he should go through with it. A voice cried out in his head: *nonsense!* He muttered, "Of course I should go through with it!"

"Say something, John?"

"No, not really…." John sighed. "Just thinking out loud…."

"Guess you got a lot to mull over, huh?"

"Yeah, well…nothing I can't handle."

The van slowed down for a lion pride and John hadn't noticed, hashing things over in his head.

He could hardly wait to join up with Ann and see the attorney — Jane's estate planning specialist. The attorney would provide instructions; i.e., how to get the parrot to open up, and divulge the money's whereabouts. Still, all *that* was elementary — John knew all about animals in general and birds in particular. Why, John knew more about birds than birds knew about birds! John Phillips would have no problem getting Cash to "sing" — instructions or no.

John suddenly went bright, a thought zipping across his mind: *The money's so in the bag…!*

\* \* \*

"OH, YEAH...! AND YOU CALL YOURSELF AN ornithologist? Let me tell you something, you need to go back to bird school! I know more about birds than you'll ever know!" Sparkle shouted into his desk telephone, his face flushed. He paused to hear the man out...and responded sharply: "No, I'm not an expert! You don't have to be an expert to know 'garbage-in, garbage-out'! The filth in this parrot's brain can be eliminated. It *can* be erased! And if you can't do it I'll find somebody who can!" He slammed down the receiver.

Sparkle was at his wit's end. Those hexing words: *Don't do it; you'll be cursed for life!*

He rifled through the directory, looking for a bird psychologist; someone who really knew their stuff. Someone who could "erase" Cash's memory once and for all!

THREE WEEKS SINCE MANHATTAN, THAT BRUTAL NIGHT IN Manhattan, and the belittling was even more brutal than the actual beating. Three weeks, and Moose was *still* tore up, his face shredded and ripped; could hardly recognize his own reflection: his right eye was almost swollen shut, face puffy and bruised, tape and gauze on his forehead, Band-Aids adorning both cheeks.

Vowing revenge, Moose worked on a plan.

A sure-fire plan!

He sat all tense at his desk, his South Hampton home posh and extensive. One way or another he'd finish this.

Unless *it* finished him first!

Moose's pen sped across the page of the pad in front of him. He already had nine other pages of notes made from the computer files, and all those pages were in shorthand....

A dull clatter shot from across the room, when Moose raised his gaze to George and Stanley pushing through the doorway. They tottered hastily across the floor, stopping before the desk.

"I'm busy...what is it?"

"Lou Gehrig Stadium is a cinch, Boss, a real pushover," said

Stanley. "Like taking candy away from a baby…!'"

"I got better things, no time for that!"

"No Boss, you don't understand," said George. "Stanley's been casing the joint, and knows exactly when and where the money will be routed. He's got all the dope!"

"That's right, Boss, just George and me — nobody else!"

"Okay, fine…but if you get pinched, you don't know me, see?"

"We wouldn't do that, Boss, not to you!" said George. "We're stand-up guys! We'd never bring you into it!"

"See that you don't!" Moose leaned back in his chair; he scratched his cheek, stroked his chin, and narrowed his eyes thoughtfully…. His tone dark, said, "Now we know how much you boys like food. Mention me to anyone and you'll NEVER EAT AGAIN!"

Their faces fell, and gulped in unison.

TWELVE THIRTY-FIVE IN THE AFTERNOON AND NOT A CLOUD in the sky. The Bronx was unseasonably hot for October, the sun beating down with a vengeance. George and Stanley sweated buckets, stuffed inside the Ford Focus like two pounds of lard in a one-pound can; they headed for the stadium.

They really couldn't afford to mess this one up.

Still, the car wasn't at all conducive, settling on that which was most accessible: a car stolen from the Bronx Court House parking lot.

Poetic justice in reverse!

George drove, and Stanley sat in the passenger seat, fighting hunger pains. He swerved into George. "There's plenty of time — turn right at the intersection and head for Mamma's Pizzeria."

"Mamma's Pizzeria…?"

"You know, just north of the ballpark!"

"Oh…that pizzeria…!"

George hung a right on Boston Road and drove past the stadium; he headed for the restaurant, Stanley moaning like a half-starved bear with a toothache. George himself wasn't hungry, the ballpark making him all but nauseous. It all started with a premonition, sensing something bad was lurking. In fact, he hardly ate a thing for breakfast: just two ice waters and four creamed coffees — heavy sugar. Two sides of sausage and eight beacon strips. Just one slice of ham and four slices of toast...plus six buttermilk pancakes — extra, extra butter. Plus one, only one 12-egg omelet smothered in cheese, inside and out....

Stanley got his food to go.

George continued on to the ballpark, Stanley peppering his fake beard with pizza.... When he got through, wiped his mouth with a napkin and tossed the box in the backseat.

The first day of the World Series and the Chicago Cubs were up against the Pittsburg Pirates, the bleachers packed. Fans showed undying support, hooting and howling and going wild in the stands; accountants too were going wild, balancing the books and squaring receipts.... George cut left on Ocean Avenue and headed for Administration, in back of the stadium. All the while George was getting cold feet, and Stanley, who had the lowdown, was brimming with confidence; he knew *when* and *where* the money would be routed, working and reworking every detail right down to the last camera.

What could go wrong?

George parked between a Jeep Cherokee and Ford Ranger, and keyed off the engine. They clamored out of the car and, donning trench coats, hurled firearms underneath their coats. They schlepped to the building, George murmuring all the way: "Somethin's not right — just not right! Somethin's gonna go wrong, I feel it. Mark my words, we're doomed!"

Stanley paid no heed, and schlepped onward.

THEY TURNED THE CORNER WITHOUT BREAKING STRIDE AND started up the stairs, the stairwell shaking and quaking. The hallway was stifling, their brimmed fedoras soaked, attached beards drenched. Water beaded their brows, sunglasses all fogged up. Sweat fell off the ends of their noses, and their chins — three chins each — were dripping.

They paused on the second floor landing, and panted. Stanley turned to George, and spoke in short, shallow gasps. "You know, George, you…really *should*…lose weight. You're…just…too fat."

"Me? How 'bout you…?" George barely caught his breath when his defenses flared.

"What about…me…? I'm not…fat!" Stanley protested.

"Oh, really…? What, five-hundred pounds isn't fat?"

"No! I'm not fat!" Stanley bristled, his jowls quivering. "I'm merely too short for my BMI, my Body-Mass Index."

"What, eight-feet…?"

"Ha, ha…that's really funny!"

"You know, Stan, you really should've been a jockey."

"A jockey…? Okay, what's the gag?"

"No gag! When you were *born* you should have been a jockey."

Stanley got all flustered. "I don't think so. A jockey weighs ninety-seven pounds."

"Isn't that what you weighed when you were born?"

"That's a good one. That's rich. At least I was born. You were *assembled* at Boeing…!"

George acted casual…as if Stanley's throwaway comment was of no importance.

Stanley produced a medicine bottle. He twisted off the cap and popped a couple pills.

"More carb blockers…?"

"Yeah…so…what of it…?"

"They don't work, that's 'what of it!'" George spoke resolutely.

"Okay, so I added a few. Woulda added a lot more without 'em…!"

George shook his head, and smirked. "Get real! What are you, five-ten…five-twenty? Whatever you are, you're at least a hundred pounds more than me! And why is *that?* Carb blockers, that's why!"

Stanley rolled his eyes, blood pressure up.

"You see, Stan, I watch what I eat. Pills aren't the answer." George lifted his head and sucked in his gut, and proudly displayed his physique — his four-hundred pound physique.

Stanley placed his hands on his well-padded hips, and snorted. "Well, thank you Dr. George.... So what exactly do *you* weigh? Still three-ninety...?

"I'm four-hundred."

"Ah, so you gained ten pounds."

"No, I lost ten pounds!"

"Sorry George, that's not how it works. You gained ten pounds."

"I lost ten pounds. Here's how. I upped my baseline...I *raised* my allotted weight twenty pounds. And since I *should* weigh fourten, I lost —"

"I get it! I get it!" Stanley jerked his gaze to the upper landing, his nerves all bottled up. "C'mon, let's get this over with."

What did it matter anyways, a hundred pounds here or there — at least *not* to Stanley. George, on the other hand, was tired of hearing *fat is fat* and five-hundred pounds is no different than four-hundred. George worked hard at keeping his weight down, and deserved credit.

Two roly-polies tottered wall to wall, like elephants crossing the veldt. The hallways were void of people, and, for good reason: apart from the treasury department, everyone had had the week off — just another detail figured into it.

THE ROOM WAS CLEAN AS A HOUND'S TOOTH, ALL BECAUSE of one woman — Winifred McNabb.

People just called her Fred.

Fred the Cleaning Lady was a skinny old woman with gray hair streaked with white and tied back in a severe bun. She wore thick glasses, her energy exceeding age; especially when it came to her handiwork, as Fred — downright quarrelsome and snappish — was a time bomb, ready to explode at the first sign of room-abuse.

She enjoyed the slots.

Just last weekend Fred went to Atlantic City and lost five-hundred dollars. Now, today, the first day of the *World Series* of all days, Fred was in a *really* bad mood. Especially since her utility bill was due and didn't have the money for it. If only someone, *anyone!* would aggravate her. Of course, the odds of that happening were slim to none, for the treasury people knew better.

"How am I s'posed to mop under your desk with those big, flat feet? Move 'em or lose 'em!" Fred barked at Lillian, typist. Wide-eyed and scared to death, Lillian responded as though "The General" had spoken.

*GOING...GOING...GONE!*

The ball sailed into the bleachers, fans jumping to their feet and giving it up for Scott Ryan and the Pittsburg Pirates.

People were enjoying the ballpark, the day sunny and bright — not a cloud in the sky. Conversely, the Treasury Room was bleak and wildly dark, where Kenneth Jordan — the man in charge — had just completed his Profits and Loss statement. Suddenly the door pelted inward, a hail of bullets dinging the entryway, shard wood decorating the floor, dust everywhere. Two gun wielding miscreants waddled inside, their firearms anchored in fat. They stood in the central aisle and fired calmly and quickly, bullets spraying into light fixtures and surveillance cameras, shells scattering about. They reloaded several times but never at the same time, people jerking backwards, dropping to the floor and scurrying under desks.

Fred stood rigid in wordless surprise, her face masked in a homicidal gleam. The gunmen ignored everything in general and Fred in particular, going about their duties in earnest, as if trying to demonstrate that they were worthy of this task and carrying it out to the best of their abilities. All the while Fred, thinking she'd died and gone to heaven, had gotten her wish.... Once the gunfire had ended, a piece of plaster fell from above, bopping her on the noggin. She groaned, and slowly looked up, when yet another piece struck her forehead, clouding her glasses. Her head aching, glasses cloudy, Fred choked her mop in a vertical hold and, letting out a biting shrill, charged the two thugs.

175

George and Stanley were blown away, their focus blurred. For all intense and purposes they were the "dumb" in dumbfounded; the "mud" in muddled; the "flab" flabbergasted.

With mop in hand, Fred struck Stanley repeatedly over his head when George, coming to the rescue, stepped squarely on her foot. Fred stopped her assault and let out a scream that could impair hearing — as if her every phalange had shattered. The woman's agony went on and on, when George clamped his hand over her mouth. But Fred still had her teeth and knew just how to use them, chomping down like a half-starved cannibal. George yanked away his hand and scraped skin; he yelped.

Nevertheless, Fred conceded — at least for the time being. She hobbled across the linoleum to Lillian's desk, and turned about; she stared down her adversaries.

The gunmen knew just how to deal with Fred.

"On your feet — now...!" Stanley spoke uncompromisingly.

People got up one by one, their heads reeling...faces dazed: Kenneth Jordan rose slowly, fretting a hostage situation. Lillian crawled out from under her desk, her knees knocking, her frail body trembling. Angela and Ned, accountants, drew up to full heights, and Leroy — all jittery — got up slowly and cautiously, his light complexion darkly shaded.

George sensed Leroy's fear, placing his submachine gun squarely between his eyes. "The money, bring us the money — now!"

"Sure thing mister, it's all yours!" Leroy whipped out his wallet, and extended it.

George knocked the wallet to the floor with one fluid sweep of his machinegun. His patience ran thin. "The money, the money...! Get the money!" George squeezed off a burst into the ceiling, his anger well demonstrated. He shoved the barrel into the bookkeeper's cheek, the muzzle burning his face.

"Would you just leave him alone," said Jordan, "there is no money!"

Stanley confronted the man in charge. "You seem to know a lot around here, huh?" He pointed his 12-guage just inches away from Jordan's head, his finger curled around the trigger. "Then maybe you know one blast from this gun and you'll be wearin' your *insides* on your *outsides...!* Now get the money or I'll comb your hair with lead!"

Jordan placed his hands over his eyes. "So be it. Just do it and get it over with, because there is *no* money!"

Stanley froze, sensing something had gone amiss.

George winced, his ruddy complexion falling pale beneath his fake beard and freckles; he hitched up his trousers, his belly withering. A warning voice went off in George's head: *Leave and leave now!* But George paid no heed, lowering his weapon and turning the show over to Stanley.

With his gun point-blank at Jordan's head, Stanley spoke through clenched teeth. "Get the money!"

The man in-charge removed his hands from his eyes, and looked down the barrel of a shotgun. Jordan asked, "What money?"

Stanley stood a little shorter and a lot wider. "The gate...the day's receipts...! Now would you please just go and get it?" Stanley was starting to fall apart at the seams. But why should he? The money was in the room because it just was — a consequence of having worked and reworked every detail hundreds of times.... Jordan was just being stubborn.

"There is no money," Jordan insisted. "Not yet, anyhow. But the minute it arrives I'll make sure Security hands it over."

Stanley cocked his head, his throat dry and scratchy. "Don't hand me *that;* you've already got it! It was dropped off not thirty minutes ago. Now GO GET IT!"

"The money is delivered at 2:00 PM sharp; that's *why* it has yet to arrive," Jordan explained.

"No, NO, NO! That's why it's here," said Stanley, lowering his shotgun and looking at his watch. "It's 2:28."

"It's not 2:28," said Jordan, scratching his head. "Didn't you men *reset* your clocks to Daylight-Savings? It's 1:28!"

Brazenness had no more than turned to shock when their every fiber sweated an icy sweat. Reality was slow to take hold but once it had, George felt nauseous, his stomach cramped and bloated. He started to gasp convulsively, like a volcano on the verge of eruption...and began hurling all over the place — like a concrete mixer gushing.

Fred was so angry she could play horseshoes with the shoe still on the horse.

Once it was over, a hush fell over the room.

Color drained out of the thugs' faces, icy trickles slithering down their backs into underwear. Seconds later a snicker emerged from out of nowhere. Then another! And another, when the room fell into hysterics, *high-fives* doling out in earnest, as if puking was never more fun.

The thugs backed awkwardly away when, in the very act of leaving, an ear-splitting shrill echoed throughout. Fred, back in the game, ran up to Stanley and began bopping him square on the noggin with her mop. She swung wild, her mop clobbering both their skulls, Stanley bobbing and weaving, George pushing and shoving, their heads molded into their hats. They wrestled their ponderous bulk out of the room and out of the building, resigning all future capers to Moose.

# About the Author

During a 20-year tour of duty with the U.S. Marines, Richard A. White dabbled in script writing on the side. After having penned his first screenplay, Richard submitted his manuscript to a Literary Agent who, in the end, fell short of closing the deal. Rather than surrender all hope, he wrote his first novel: "Cosmic Dust." He has since expanded his book into "Cosmic Dust and the Eternal Code" — a work of exhilarating humor and characterization. Richard believes that everyone has the ability of becoming an author, an artist, or anything desired, so long as determination is at the fore.

Richard A. White was born on April 14, 1952 in Oak Park, Illinois, and was raised on the Northwest Side of Chicago, where father William provided a decent living for the family. Born number three amid five, Richard took an early interest in reading, going to the movies, and television. Among his favorite TV shows were *Sgt. Bilko, The Honeymooners,* and *Lost in Space.* He especially enjoyed *The Jack Benny Show....* As a boy, Richard aspired to becoming a comedy writer. His mother, however, had other plans, turning him into a musician instead. Still, his early years produced an accomplished composer and arranger — clarinetist and saxophonist. Having joined the US Marines in 1975, Richard worked as a musician throughout his entire hitch. Now retired, Richard takes pleasure in doing what he likes most.... Writing....

CPSIA information can be obtained at www.ICGtesting.com
Printed in the USA
LVOW08s1027310314

379650LV00003B/54/P